OTHER BOOKS BY ...

The Trident Security Series

Leather & Lace: Book 1

His Angel: Book 2

Waiting For Him: Book 3

Not Negotiable: A Novella Book 3.5

Topping The Alpha: Book 4

Watching From the Shadows: Book 5

Whiskey Tribute: A Novella Book 5.5

Tickle His Fancy: Book 6

No Way in Hell: A Steel Corp/Trident Security Crossover: Books 1 & 2

Absolving His Sins: Book 7

Option Number Three: A Novella Book 7.5

Salvaging His Soul: Book 8

The Deimos Series

Handling Haven: Special Forces: Operation Alpha: A Trident Security/Delta Force Crossover - Deimos Book 1

Cheating the Devil: Special Forces: Operation Alpha: A Trident Security/Delta Force Crossover - Deimos Book 2

The Trident Security Omega Team Series

Mountain of Evil: TS Omega Team Prequel

A Dead Man's Pulse: TS Omega Team Book 1

Forty Days & One Knight: Book 2—Coming Soon

Summer's Fall: Book 3—Coming Soon

The Doms of The Covenant Series

Double Down & Dirty Book 1

Entertaining Distraction: Book 2

Hammered & Nailed—Coming Soon

The Malone Brothers Series

Take the Money and Run: Book 1

The Devil's Spare Change: Book 2

The Ultimate Price: Book 3—Coming Soon

The Hazard Falls Series

Don't Fight It: Book 1

The Blackhawk Security Series

Tuff Enough: Book 1—Coming December 2018

Stand Alone Novels

The Road to Solace

Special Projects

The Trident Security Coloring Book

Word Search For Warriors: Authors For a Cause

Shaded with Love Volume 5: Coloring Book for a Cause

Cooking with Love: Shaded with Love Volume 6

First Chapters: Foreplay Volume One

First Chapters: Foreplay Volume Two

First Chapters: Foreplay Volume Three

PRAISE FOR SAMANTHA A. COLE

"I am new to Samantha Cole and I just wonder how I missed her? Wow she really nailed this! This was sweet and naughty at the same time. I really enjoyed reading about Grayson, Remington, and Abigail."

— SNOWBUNNY1977

"I loved this book! I really liked these characters and watching their story unfold. I laughed, cried, and wanted to slap someone silly. I was quickly swept in the story and didn't want to put the book down. I can't wait to read the other books in this series!"

— LOVES TO READ

"What can I say about Samantha Cole's Double Down and Dirty? Very few authors leave me wanting for words. I love it or hate it. But Samantha's writing leaves me speechless every time. And in a very good way. Her latest Double Down and Dirty did not disappoint either . . . If you have not read this (or honestly anything else Samantha Cole has written) run do not walk and get it. Her heroes are totally Alpha and her heroines are spunky and willing to protect those they love. You will not be disappointed."

— CAT W.

"Now the fun really starts and Cole works her magic. The seduction is slow and sweet sending tingles down the reader's spine ... romantic and intriguing. Cole's books are much more than romance, it is about respect, friendships, family and being ethical and moral . . .Cole's books show a depth to her characters and story lines that are growing with each book she writes. Cole's growth as a story teller and writer has been amazing to watch unfold moving from the simple to more complex story lines adding in more characters and growing the Trident/Covenant world.

— WORDSAPLENTY

DOUBLE DOWN & DIRTY

DOMS OF THE COVENANT BOOK ONE

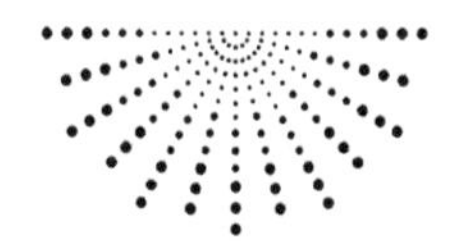

SAMANTHA A. COLE

SUSPENSEFUL SEDUCTION PUBLISHING

Double Down & Dirty

Suspenseful Seduction Publishing

Cover designed by Judi Perkins of Concierge Literary Design —www.cldesignsky.com
Editing by Eve Arroyo—www.evearroyo.com

ISBN: 978-1948822169

To Jessica L. and Julie G. who have been with me since almost the beginning of this amazing, literary journey. Love you gals!

WHO'S WHO AND THE HISTORY OF TRIDENT SECURITY AND THE COVENANT

***While not every character is in every book, these are the ones with the most mentions throughout the series. This guide will help keep readers straight about who's who.

Trident Security (TS) is a private investigative and military agency, co-owned by Ian and Devon Sawyer. With governmental and civilian contracts, the company got its start when the brothers and a few of their teammates from SEAL Team Four retired to the private sector. The original six-man team is referred to as the Sexy Six-Pack, as they were dubbed by Kristen Sawyer, née Anders, or the Alpha Team. Trident had since expanded and former members of the military and law enforcement have been added to the staff. The company is located on a guarded compound, which was a former import/export company cover for a drug trafficking operation in Tampa, Florida. Three warehouses on the property were converted into large apartments, the TS offices, gym, and bunkrooms. There is also an obstacle course, a Main Street shooting gallery, a helicopter pad, and more features necessary for training and missions.

In addition to the security business, there is a fourth

warehouse that now houses an elite BDSM club, co-owned by Devon, Ian, and their cousin, Mitch Sawyer, who is the manager. A lot of time and money has gone into making The Covenant the most sought after membership in the Tampa/St. Petersburg area and beyond. Members are thoroughly vetted before being granted access to the elegant club.

There are currently over fifty Doms who have been appointed Dungeon Masters (DMs), and they rotate two or three shifts each throughout the month. At least four DMs are on duty at all times at various posts in the pit, playrooms, and the new garden, with an additional one roaming around. Their job is to ensure the safety of all the submissives in the club. They step in if a sub uses their safeword and the Dom in the scene doesn't hear or heed it, and make sure the equipment used in scenes isn't harming the subs.

The Covenant's security team takes care of everything else that isn't scene-related, and provides safety for all members and are essentially the bouncers. With the recent addition of the garden, and more private, themed rooms, the owners have expanded their self-imposed limit of 350 members. The fire marshal had approved them for 500 when the warehouse-turned-kink club first opened, but the cousins had intentionally kept that number down to maintain an elite status. Now with more room, they are increasing the membership to 500, still under the new maximum occupancy of 720.

Between Trident Security and The Covenant there's plenty of romance, suspense, and steamy encounters. Come meet the Sexy Six-Pack, their friends, family, and teammates.

The Sexy Six-Pack (Alpha Team)
and Their Significant Others

- Ian "Boss-man" Sawyer: Devon and Nick's brother; retired Navy SEAL; co-owner of Trident Security and The Covenant; husband/Dom of Angelina (Angel).
- Devon "Devil Dog" Sawyer: Ian and Nick's brother; retired Navy SEAL; co-owner of Trident Security and The Covenant; husband/Dom of Kristen; father of John Devon "JD."
- Ben "Boomer" Michaelson: retired Navy SEAL; explosives and ordnance specialist; husband/Dom of Katerina; son of Rick and Eileen.
- Jake "Reverend" Donovan: retired Navy SEAL; temporarily assigned to run the West Coast team; sniper; fiancé/Dom of Nick; brother of Mike; Whip Master at The Covenant.
- Brody "Egghead" Evans: retired Navy SEAL; computer specialist; husband/Dom of Fancy.
- Marco "Polo" DeAngelis: retired Navy SEAL; communications specialist and back up helicopter pilot; husband/Dom of Harper; father to Mara.
- Nick "Junior" Sawyer: Ian and Devon's brother; current Navy SEAL; fiancé/submissive of Jake.
- Kristen "Ninja-girl" Sawyer: author of romance/suspense novels; wife/submissive of Devon; mother of "JD."
- Angelina "Angie/Angel" Sawyer: graphic artist; wife/submissive of Ian.
- Katerina "Kat" Michaelson: dog trainer for law enforcement and private agencies; wife/submissive of Boomer.
- Millicent "Harper" DeAngelis: lawyer; wife/submissive of Marco; mother of Mara.
- Francine "Fancy" Maguire: baker; wife/submissive of Brody.

Extended Family, Friends, and Associates of the Sexy Six-Pack

- Mitch Sawyer: Cousin of Ian, Devon, and Nick; co-owner/manager of The Covenant.
- T. Carter: US spy and assassin; works for covert agency Deimos; Dom of Jordyn.
- Jordyn Alvarez: US spy and assassin; member of covert agency Deimos; submissive of Carter.
- Parker Christiansen: owner of New Horizons Construction; husband/Dom of Shelby; adoptive father of Franco and Victor.
- Shelby Christiansen: stay-at-home mom; two-time cancer survivor; wife/submissive of Parker; adoptive mother of Franco and Victor.
- Curt Bannerman: retired Navy SEAL; owner of Halo Customs, a motorcycle repair and detail shop; husband of Dana; stepfather of Ryan, Taylor, Justin, and Amanda. Lives in Iowa.
- Dana Prichard-Bannerman: teacher; widow of retired SEAL Eric Prichard; wife of Curt; mother of Ryan, Taylor, Justin, and Amanda. Lives in Iowa.
- Jenn "Baby-girl" Mullins: college student; goddaughter of Ian; "niece" of Devon, Brody, Jake, Boomer, and Marco; father was a Navy SEAL; parents murdered.
- Mike Donovan: owner of the Irish pub, Donovan's; brother of Jake.
- Charlotte "Mistress China" Roth: Parole officer; Domme and Whip Master at The Covenant.
- Travis "Tiny" Daultry: former professional football player; head of security at The Covenant and Trident compound; occasional bodyguard for TS.

- Doug "Bullseye" Henderson: retired Marine; head of the Personal Protection Division of TS.
- Rick and Eileen Michaelson: Boomer's parents; guardians of Alyssa. Rick is a retired Navy SEAL.
- Charles "Chuck" and Marie Sawyer: Ian, Devon, and Nick's parents. Charles is a self-made real estate billionaire. Marie is a plastic surgeon involved with Operation Smile.
- Dr. Roxanne London: pediatrician; Domme/wife (Mistress Roxy) of Kayla; Whip Master at Covenant.
- Kayla London: social worker; submissive/wife of Roxanne.
- Grayson and Remington Mann: twins; owners of Black Diamond Records; Doms/fiancés of Abigail; members of The Covenant.
- Abigail Turner: personal assistant at Black Diamond Records; submissive/fiancée of Gray and Remi.
- Chase Dixon: retired Army Ranger; owner of Blackhawk Security; associate of TS.
- Reggie Helm: lawyer for TS and The Covenant; Dom of Colleen.
- Alyssa Wagner: teenager saved by Jake from an abusive father; lives with Rick and Eileen Michaelson.
- Carl Talbot: college professor; Dom and Whip Master at The Covenant.

The Omega Team and Their Significant Others

- Cain "Shades" Foster: retired Secret Service agent.

- Tristan "Duracell" McCabe: retired Army Special Forces
- Logan "Cowboy" Reese: retired Marine Special Forces; former prisoner of war.
- Valentino "Romeo" Mancini: retired Army Special Forces; former FBI Hostage Rescue Team (HRT) member.
- Darius "Batman" Knight: retired Navy SEAL.
- Kip "Skipper" Morrison: retired Army; former LAPD SWAT sniper.
- Lindsey "Costello" Abbott: retired Marine; sniper.

Trident Support Staff

- Colleen McKinley-Helm: office manager of TS; submissive of Reggie.
- Tempest "Babs" Van Buren: retired Air Force helicopter pilot; TS mechanic.
- Russell Adams: retired Navy; assistant TS mechanic.
- Nathan Cook: former computer specialist with the National Security Agency (NSA).

Members of Law Enforcement

- Larry Keon: Assistant Director of the FBI.
- Frank Stonewall: Special Agent in Charge of the Tampa FBI.
- Calvin Watts: Leader of the FBI HRT in Tampa.

The K9s of Trident

- Beau: An orphaned Lab/Pit mix, rescued by Ian.

Now a trained K9 who has more than earned his spot on the Alpha Team.

- Spanky: A rescued Bullmastiff with a heart of gold, owned by Parker and Shelby.
- Jagger: A rescued Rottweiler trained as an assistance/service animal for Russell.
- FUBAR: A Belgian Malinois who failed aggressive guard dog training. Adopted by Babs.

CHAPTER ONE

"Abby, hold all my calls."

"Yes, Mr. Mann." Startled by his sudden appearance, scowling face, and barked order, Abigail's heart was pounding as her boss, Grayson Mann, strode into his office, without a backward glance, and slammed the door shut. Well, actually, he was one of her bosses—the other was his fraternal twin brother, Remington, who was currently out of town on a business trip to Miami. It was just after seven-thirty in the morning on the twenty-first floor of Black Diamond Records in Tampa, Florida, and she hadn't expected Gray in before nine today. He'd been scheduled to attend a breakfast meeting with the record label's branding development team on the third floor. Gray and Remi were the producers of some of the hottest bands and solo artists in the world. No genres were excluded—performers of rock, country, classical, rap, easy-listening, gospel, and more had found international stardom thanks to the Mann brothers.

Abigail had been the CEOs' personal secretary for six months now after working for the vice president of marketing for a year. Remi and Gray's longtime secretary,

Liz Carpenter, had resigned to go work for her husband's booming law practice, and had recommended Abigail as her replacement after the two had become friends.

She'd been shocked at the huge promotion. While she loved the increase in pay and benefits, part of her wanted her old job back. Not that her new bosses were difficult to work for, because they weren't. The problem was they were gorgeous—total dreamboats—and she tended to be flustered around them. Both were well over six feet tall, with solid physiques, dark brown hair, and adorable dimples, but that's where the similarities ended. Remi had soft brown eyes, while Gray's hazel ones were harsher—not that he was mean or anything, he just didn't relax or smile as often as his brother did. Why they'd given her the job as their secretary when she always seemed to stutter in their combined presence was beyond her. But once they were behind their respective, closed office doors, she did her duties with complete efficiency, so they obviously overlooked her flaws.

While Gray remained in his office, Abigail finished off a stack of correspondence Remi had left on her desk before departing for Miami late yesterday afternoon. She'd just sent the last letter to the printer, when the door to the CEOs' reception area opened, and Chad Crawford walked in. The head of the recording studio division was dressed in his usual khakis and a green polo shirt with the Black Diamond Records' signature BDR logo on it. He also wore a huge smile as he sat on the edge of her desk.

"Hey, gorgeous. How are things going today?"

Abigail blushed. Chad was sweet, good-looking, and a huge flirt—at least he was with her. He'd asked her out on a date when she'd first started working at BDR, but she'd turned him down, not wanting to have an office romance. Although his disappointment had been clear, they'd ended up becoming good friends. He even consulted her now about what to wear or where to go on his dates, and she hoped one day he'd find Ms. Right, because he really deserved her—she just wasn't Abigail.

"So far so good. Just finishing up a few things. How was the blind date last night?"

He rolled his eyes. "I was ready to run ten minutes into it after she started planning our wedding."

Abigail's hand froze over the paper she was about to pluck from the printer. "Oh, my God! Are you serious? What kind of woman does that?"

"Yup. A desperate one, I guess." He winked at her again. "You know, one of these days you should put me out of my dating misery. Oh, that's right, you don't date."

She rolled her eyes. "I date. I just don't advertise that I date."

"Uh-huh. When was the last time—"

Whatever his question was, it ended up being cut off by Grayson's door flying open, and the man storming out into the reception area. His face became thunderous, his beautiful, hazel eyes flaring in annoyance at the sight of Chad sitting on her desk. "Crawford, is there a reason you're here, other than to flirt with my secretary? If not, get out."

Oh, boy, he really is in a bad mood, Abigail thought.

With an apologetic glance at Abigail, Chad leapt up. "Uh . . . sorry, boss. I . . . uh . . . just wanted you to know we're done with the final mixing of Aurora's latest album. She really knocked it out of the park with this one."

Aurora Locke was one of Black Diamond Records' top selling artists of all time. She was also a stuck-up bitch, in Abigail's opinion. The twenty-six-year-old woman had no concept of what the word humble meant, among other things. She treated everyone at BDR like they were miles beneath her feet, with the exception of Grayson and Remington—who also happened to be her boyfriends for the past three months. Yup, the Mann twins shared their women, a concept Abigail knew nothing about, other than what she'd read in the fictional romance books she loved. She'd always been too embarrassed to ask Liz what she knew about it, and there was no way she was asking either of the two men. That was far too personal. She was their secretary and nothing more. But that didn't stop her from having dreams of being sandwiched between the hunky twins.

"Give it to Tessa to approve."

While Abigail hid her surprise to that statement, Chad's shock was clear as day, his jaw almost hitting the floor. Tessa Mann was the twins' younger cousin and in charge of all new album releases the CEOs didn't handle personally.

At six foot three, Gray towered over the shorter man by a good six inches. His eyes narrowed as he placed a thick file on top of Abigail's in-box. "Problem?" he barked.

"Uh, n-no, boss. I just figured you or Remi would handle Aurora's release."

Gray turned on his heel and strode toward his office. "You figured wrong."

The door slammed shut, and Chad raised his brow and whistled at Abigail. "Trouble in paradise?"

"I have no idea." And even if she did, Abigail would never discuss it with her bosses' employees. What happened in this office, stayed in this office. "But it's not my concern—nor yours." She reached for the file Gray had left. "Looks like I'll be busy for the rest of the morning."

Chad headed for the door leading out to the main reception area. "And I've got to track down Tessa now. See you later, my little chick-a-dee."

Shaking her head, Abigail let out a light chuckle. He really was a sweet man; she just didn't feel an attraction to him. At least not like the one she felt for Gray and Remi. Those two men only had to walk into the room, and her heart beat out of control, her mouth went dry—which was the complete opposite of what happened between her legs—and butterflies took flight in her stomach. But she was far from their "type" of woman, if the celebrity gossip magazines were to believed. Those women were just like their current girlfriend, Aurora —tall, blonde, skinny, with huge tits. That was a far cry from mousy, brown-haired Abigail's five-foot-six, size twelve frame. Even her 38-Bs were lacking. She wasn't even close to red-carpet material, so therefore, both the twins were way out of her league.

The rest of the morning flew by with Abigail answering a few dozen phone calls and putting out several figurative fires, in addition to all her other duties. It wasn't unusual to have people calling, demanding to speak to one or the other CEO, with a so-called emergency. Part of being a good, efficient personal secretary was knowing which ones truly needed her bosses' attention and which problems could be easily handled by the appropriate department heads. Abigail had become an expert at weeding the latter out and, today, had successfully avoided bothering Gray behind his closed door.

It was twenty minutes before noon when the glass door to the executive offices flew open and Aurora Locke burst in, sheer fury written all over her face. As always, she was dressed as if she were going on stage at any moment. Who wore black, leather pants, thigh-high boots, and a see-through shirt over a satin bra to an office in the middle of a Tuesday morning? *Someone with a body to pull it off,* Abigail thought wryly as she stood up quickly. "Can I help you, Ms. Locke?"

Without a glance or word to the secretary, Aurora stormed into Gray's office, slamming the door back against the wall where it bounced closed again, but not completely, which meant Abigail could hear every word. The woman's hard voice was a far cry from the melodious one her fans heard daily over the radio. "You son of a fucking bitch! I've been calling your cell phone all fucking morning! Why the hell were all my things delivered to me this morning in fucking cardboard boxes? Does Remi know about this?"

Gray's voice was also hard, but in contrast, calm, low, and deadly. "Of course he knows, Aurora. He also knows you spent Sunday night in another man's bed." Something light slapped down on his desk. "The private detective didn't get your good side in these photos, but it really doesn't matter, now does it? They're not exactly *People* magazine material—more like *Playboy*."

"Holy shit," Abigail muttered to herself as she stepped over to subtly close Gray's door the rest of the way. As much as she wanted to eavesdrop, she'd heard enough to know the other woman would no longer be sharing a bed with the twins. And the last thing she wanted was someone else to walk in and hear the screeching and sputtering from Aurora, which although still audible, was now sufficiently muffled.

Sitting back at her desk, she couldn't help the perverse satisfaction that came over her knowing the snotty bitch had fallen from the "current girlfriend" column to the "ex" column. Maybe the next one would be a lot friendlier.

GRAY WATCHED as Aurora marched out his office, madder than a wet hen. He was certain once her anger at being booted from their personal lives subsided, she'd be groveling and begging for them to take her back. And that wasn't happening. While he and Remi had known their ménage with the superstar would one day fizzle out, like they all did, they hadn't expected it to be so soon. And definitely not because she'd been cheating on them with her fucking bodyguard of all fucking people.

Leaning forward, he punched a button on his desk phone. "Abby, please get Ian Sawyer on the line for me."

"Yes, sir."

He sat back in his chair and tried to ignore how those two words flowing from his secretary's pretty, plump lips made him feel. While he and Remi had no trouble dating their contracted artists, the employees of Black Diamond Records were off limits. And damn, didn't that suck when it came to sweet Abby Turner. Everyone but the twins called her Abigail—Gray and Remi preferred the shortened moniker, and she'd never suggested she was unhappy with it.

With sensual, womanly curves, Abby made his dick twitch just by entering the room. But his brother and he had agreed long before she came to work for them that office romances—or brief trysts—were not an option. They didn't want to put any woman through the company's gossip mill; they valued their employees and would hate to see anyone hurt for being involved with the big bosses.

It wasn't well-known, but his and Remi's sexual proclivities veered toward the dark side. He was certain the beautiful, young thing who ran their offices with excellence would flee into the night, screaming if she knew what they wanted to do to her. Being Dominants in the BDSM lifestyle for years, they enjoyed sexual play that tended to be frowned upon by mainstream society, although many people's misconceptions had changed in recent years thanks to popular romance novels featuring the subject. In fact, Ian's sister-in-law, Kristen, was a famous author whose last few best sellers took place in a BDSM club similar to the one the Sawyer brothers owned, where Gray and Remi also happened to be members. The Covenant was the top, private lifestyle club in the Tampa/St. Petersburg area, and the elite membership was contingent on a strict background check.

"Ian Sawyer is on line three for you, sir."

God, what he wouldn't give for her to call him Sir during a scene where he and Remi made her cum over and over. Pushing the delicious thought from his mind, he picked up the phone. "Ian?"

The Covenant and Trident Security co-owner's voice rumbled over the line. "What's up, Gray? Did you take care of that problem?"

"This morning. Thank Boomer for getting those photos to me so quickly. Aurora is officially a thing of the past." He'd suspected the woman had been cheating on them for a week before finally calling in a favor and having her followed. Ian's employee and teammate had gotten up close and personal with a long-range, zoom camera lens the vultures who made up the paparazzi would drool over. The Trident operative had come to the house Gray shared with his brother last night with the 8 x 10 glossies. Ten minutes later, Gray had been packing up all the woman's shit she'd left at the house and sent it by private courier this morning with a simple "fuck you" note attached. Petty, yes, but damn, it'd felt good. There was a list of things he wouldn't tolerate in his woman and cheating was at the top, second only to disobedience when it came to safety.

"Good, and I will. I've already removed her from the club's approved guest list." If Aurora had been an actual member of the club, it wouldn't have been so easy to blackball her, but she'd only been approved as a guest of Remi and Gray. Because of her guest status, she hadn't been allowed to play on the premises, but it had let them explore possibilities for scenes at home with her. "If it's any consolation, my wife says most of the submissives hated her, and as a result, won't be buying any more of her music." He paused, then added wryly, "Well, since that's a loss of money for you, too, I guess that's not anything to celebrate. Anyway, I spoke to Chase Dixon last night, and he'll be firing the guard—he's as strict as I am about guards messing with clients. And on that note, Dev and I have decided to expand the personal protection section of the business, so we won't be contracting out the bodyguards as much anymore. One of Chase's men, Doug Henderson, has signed on to oversee that division with us."

"Glad to hear business is booming."

"Always a good thing, right? So, are you and Remi going to be attending the races next Saturday? We're trying to get a head count."

Gray laughed for the first time all morning. December's theme night was coinciding with the opening of the new wing at The Covenant. While the members knew a few basics of what was being added, a week from Saturday was the big reveal combined with the annual Christmas party. And to celebrate, A Night at the Reindeer Races was the theme. He could only imagine what that entailed, but like everyone else, he'd been left to speculate until then. "Yeah, we'll be there. I'm sure we'll find a single subbie to keep us entertained for the evening."

"A new training class is finishing up, and they'll be available as of this weekend, so I'm sure you'll find some poor woman to fall for your charm." The man's amused grin could almost be heard over the phone. "Listen, I've got to run. If there's nothing else . . ."

"Yeah, we're good. Send the bill to our residence."

"You got it. Talk to you soon."

Hanging up the phone, Gray spun his chair around and stared out over the Tampa Riverwalk. Behind him, he heard the door open, and Abigail cleared her throat before speaking. "Do you need anything before I go to lunch, sir?"

He didn't turn back to face her. If he did, he'd be hard as a rock within seconds. "Abby, how many times have I asked you to call me Gray when we're alone in the office?" He wanted to hear her call him by his first name as much as he wanted to hear her use the title Sir in a D/s setting. But, alas, he'd have to settle for the former because the latter would never happen.

"I—um—I . . . a f-few times, sir . . . I mean, Gray."

A satisfied smile spread across his face. "Thank you. Have a nice lunch."

"Th-thank you, sir . . . I mean, thank you, Gray."

The door shut and the brief sunshine that had brightened his world dimmed again.

CHAPTER TWO

Leaving his carry-on suitcase and laptop at the foot of the stairs in the foyer, Remington Mann went in search of his brother and found him in the den. Sitting on the couch with his feet on the ottoman, Gray had a tumbler filled with ice and whiskey in his hand, as he stared at the blaze in the gas fireplace. The flat-screen TV above it was showing the latest CNN news report, but the sound was off. Instead, soulful jazz filtered through the surround sound speakers. Remi helped himself to a glass of the Jack Daniel's Monogram Tennessee Whiskey before plopping down in his favorite, brown, leather recliner. He took a sip of the $750 liquor and let the smooth, smoky flavor pleasure his taste buds before swallowing, welcoming the familiar burn in his stomach. "So . . . twenty-seven voice mail messages from Aurora. I really wish there was a 'delete all' feature on the damn phone."

Gray snorted. "She knew better than to pull that shit with me. You're too soft, brother. She knows there's no way I'll take her back if you won't."

It was true, so Remi didn't feel insulted. Gray had always

been the more reserved and stoic one of the two men, while his younger-by-one-minute sibling was the relaxed, more sociable one. They complemented each other like yin and yang. "Well, then she doesn't stand a chance. She knew the rules from day one."

"And I knew from day one she wasn't long term, so let's move on. How was Miami?"

Remi rolled his eyes and took another sip of whiskey. "I swear, I really hate dealing with the parents of minors. Josh Halstead's mother thinks her son walks on water. Did you know she wanted us to pay for weekly manicures and pedicures for both her *and* the kid? He's fucking fourteen for Christ's sake. What fourteen-year-old boy, gay or straight, wants a fucking mani/pedi on a weekly basis?" They'd found the teenager on YouTube and knew they had to snatch him up before someone else did. He had the looks, talent, and charisma to go far in the music business. Hopefully, he'd be one of the kids who didn't let it go to his head and become a publicist's nightmare. Black Diamond Records had their fair share of those, as did every other recording empire.

"I take it that didn't make it into the contract." Gray still hadn't taken his eyes off the mesmerizing flickering of the fire.

"Nope, and about ninety-five percent of the other shit she wanted didn't make it in either. She finally signed on the dotted line when I stood and made a beeline for the elevator. She realized I was serious about not taking the kid on, no matter how good a singer he is, unless it was on our terms. I told Tessa to put him on the recording schedule starting next Tuesday with the playlist we'd decided on." Many artists didn't write their own music and many song writers didn't record their own songs. BDR maintained a long list of previously unrecorded works that would hopefully be in the Top 40 someday with the right singer.

He eyed Gray. Something else was on his mind, and it wasn't Aurora. They'd both known the singer would one day be a thing of the past in their private lives. While she'd been fun and adventurous in the beginning, her elitist attitude toward others had started to grate on both of them. She also hadn't been a true submissive, although, she did enjoy playing in the BDSM lifestyle. Some people got off on the slap and tickle part of it, but other submissives needed more than that—they needed the opportunity to completely submit to their Dom or Domme. "Anything else happen today I need to know about?"

There was a long pause before Gray looked at him. "Crawford was sniffing around Abby again."

Ah. Remi should have known. "Chad's a good friend of hers. Yeah, he flirts, but he doesn't stand a chance with her. I overheard her talking to Liz one day, and there's no attraction there for her. And we agreed we wouldn't touch her, so therefore, she's not ours to be jealous over. Someday she'll meet some asshole she likes, and we won't have a say in the matter." That bothered him as much as it bothered Gray. He tilted his head and stared at his brother. "Unless you want to change your mind. You know I have no problems breaking the unwritten rule of not getting involved with employees when it comes to Abby. She's different from the others."

"She's too sweet and innocent," his twin replied, running a hand through his hair. "If we tried to bring her into our world, we'd lose her as our secretary *and* as our woman. I'm not willing to risk that. She's the best secretary we've ever had, and that includes Liz, who was a saint putting up with our shit for as long as she did."

"So stop grumbling every time a guy flirts with Abby."

"I'm not grumbling."

Remi stood and downed the last of his whiskey. "Yes, you

are, brother. And I'm not in the mood for it. If you need me, I'll be relaxing in the hot tub."

"Whatever. Oh, before I forget. Ian is trying to get a headcount for the grand opening of the new wing next week." Gray raised a questioning eyebrow. "We going?"

"Oh, yeah. I'm dying to see what fun stuff the Sawyers have thought up—should be very entertaining. I also heard a new batch of submissives are finishing up their training sessions. Maybe one will catch our eye." He didn't doubt it. Since Marco DeAngelis and Brody Evans had both met their significant others, they were no longer free to tag-team, which meant there was one less ménage duo for the single submissives to choose from. They'd be happy to hear the Mann twins were back on the available list for threesome scenes.

Striding out to the lanai, he stripped off all his clothes and flipped on the power switch for the hot tub before climbing in. Between the lush vegetation and secure perimeter wall, he could sit out here buck-naked and not have to worry about being seen or giving the paparazzi a photo opportunity. Yet, he was still able to have a great view.

This was the life. Their $8.5 million, six-bedroom mansion was located in Bellaire, overlooking Tampa Bay and the city lights twinkling across the water. When they'd been looking to purchase a home in either Clearwater Beach or Bellaire, it hadn't taken them long to decide on a property that backed up to the bay as opposed to looking out over the gulf. One had beautiful sunrises, while the other, stunning sunsets. But with the bay, they had a dock for a boat and jet ski launches. And it wasn't a far walk to the beach. Remi did it several times a week before taking a run down the sandy shoreline. Once in a while, he just sat there, watching the sun go down as dolphins played in the water. The peacefulness of it all calmed him just the way the D/s lifestyle did. It was a way for him to leave all the stress of running a competitive, international business behind and just relax, soothing his mind, body, and soul.

Remi reached over and pushed a button that activated the outdoor speakers and the same relaxing music Gray had on floated through the air. Adjusting a few of the jets, he was soon enjoying the pulsating water hitting his upper and lower back in all the right spots. He'd forgone turning on the outdoor lights in favor of being able to see the millions of stars overhead. This was definitely the life. So why did it feel like something . . . or *someone* was missing?

"I'M SORRY. BLACK DIAMOND RECORDS' employees do not comment on the CEOs' personal lives. Please contact their publicist." Abigail hung up the phone, resisting the urge to slam the handset down on its cradle. Over the past two days, on top of her routine, business phone calls, the paparazzi had been doing their best to try and get a quote from either Remi or Gray about Aurora Locke's newly single status. The news and ensuing speculation was all over social media and the news outlets. While most of the reporters knew they'd never get past the secretary, that hadn't stopped them from trying. Thankfully, BDR had a fully-staffed, media relations division, which handled the Mann brothers' publicity, in addition to that of their clients.

Glancing at the clock, Abigail noticed it was a little after twelve. No wonder her stomach had been growling. While she was entitled to leave for a forty-five-minute lunch, she often ate at her desk with her e-reader, especially when she had the office to herself. Even with all their combined meetings, it was rare for Remi and Gray to both be gone for the entire day unless they were out of town. In addition to the main headquarters, they had offices in New York, Chicago, Las Vegas, and, of course, Los Angeles. With those exciting cities, she often wondered why they'd picked Tampa as their home base, but since she benefited from it, she didn't question it.

Punching a speed dial button on her phone, she told the receptionist out front she was putting on the call forwarding for her lunch. After completing that, she stood and locked the main door to the executive suite. She'd have complete silence to dive into *Velvet Vixen,* Kristen Anders's latest book she'd been dying to read since it had been released a few weeks ago. She loved that the author's books were all set in Tampa; it felt like the characters were real and living in her hometown. The only reason Abigail hadn't started the romance/suspense novel yet was she had several favorite, must-read authors. And it seemed like they'd all published their latest books at the same time, so she was reading them in the order they'd appeared on her device. Today, she was going to find out what Ms. Anders had in store for Master Zach. BDSM books had become her secret, guilty pleasure over the past few years.

It didn't take long for her partially-eaten, tuna salad sandwich to be forgotten as she fell into the digital pages of the book. Master Zach was spanking Priscilla for the first time after she'd disobeyed him, and Abigail found herself getting as turned on as the lucky heroine. Her nipples puckered and her clit throbbed with need as her pussy grew damp. Her mind drifted from the story to her being bent over her desk, her skirt pulled up to her waist, as Gray and Remi took turns slapping her bare ass.

Holy shit! She needed to give herself some relief if she was going to make it through the day. But how? She couldn't get off where she sat. Even though for another half hour, the receptionist should stop anyone from coming down the hallway to where they'd be able to see Abigail at her desk through the floor to ceiling glass windows and door, she couldn't risk it. And the ladies' room in the hall was shared with three other women from the outer offices, so that was a no-go too.

Abigail's gaze went to Remi's office. Neither of the CEOs would be back for the rest of the day, as they'd both had full schedules. With the locked door that led to the main reception area and the lock on the office door, she could masturbate and relieve the needy ache between her legs and be back out at her desk with no one being the wiser.

Hesitating, she bit her bottom lip. She couldn't do it, could she? It was her boss's office of all places . . . her totally hot, drool-worthy, panty-dropping boss's office. And that had her clenching her thighs together. *Way to talk yourself out of it, Abigail.*

She wouldn't have to worry about anyone coming in because the only people who had passkeys to the executive suite were her, Remi, Gray, and the head of their security team. Since that man had been here earlier in the morning to talk to Remi, and knew the CEOs would be gone for the rest of the day, he wouldn't be back unless it was an emergency. The men took their security seriously, keeping their multi-million dollar prospects and current clients' files locked up tight. Even the cleaning staff didn't have a key. Abigail let them in after she arrived each morning at 7:45. They would then spend the next forty-five minutes vacuuming, dusting, and emptying the trash from both offices and her reception area. They'd be gone before either of the twins came in at 8:30 or later.

Pushing her chair away from the desk, she paused one more time before throwing caution to the wind. She double-checked the lock on the outer door then grabbed her e-reader and hurried into Remi's office. Shutting the door, she engaged the lock before she changed her mind or ran out of time. Inhaling deeply, she detected the enticing aroma of Remi's expensive aftershave, the lemon wood spray the cleaners used, and the leather couch and executive desk chair.

Standing next to the couch, Abigail hiked her suit's skirt up to her hips and sat down. She held her e-reader in her left hand as her right dropped to her wide-spread legs, pushed aside her panties, and fingered her wet pussy. *Pussy.* That was a word she would never say out loud to anyone, but in her sexual fantasies—fantasies that included Gray and Remi—they loved it when she talked dirty to them.

As she ran her fingers over her clit and through her folds, she read two more paragraphs of the scene between Master Zach and Pricilla before they were replaced by her and Gray in her mind. She put the digital device on the couch beside her.

Abigail closed her eyes as Remi joined his brother in Gray's office with Abby bent over the desk, her ass bare to them.

"You're our naughty secretary, aren't you, Abby?" Master Remi asked. "And naughty secretaries get punished, don't they?"

She swallowed hard at the unyielding, yet seductive tone of his voice. "Yes, Master Remi, I'm so naughty. I need to be punished for losing that important file you needed."

"Most definitely," Master Gray told her. "Maybe ten spanks will remind you to be more responsible, Abby."

"T-ten, Sir?"

"Yes, ten. Unless you want more than that?"

Before she could answer him, his flat hand landed on her right ass cheek with a smack that echoed in the room, followed quickly by Master Remi's palm on her left.

"Ohhhh. Yes, Sirs. Spank me. Please spank me so I don't forget next time."

The fantasy continued to play out in Abigail's mind as her fingers moved faster and harder over her clit.

After they were done spanking her, they laid her naked on the desk. Remi pulled her hips until her sore ass was at the edge. He dropped his dress pants, revealing his glorious, erect cock. As he lined it up with her vagina, she turned her head to see Gray had also stripped and his dick was just as impressive as his brother's. He wrapped her hand around it and showed her how to pump him as Remi thrust forward, impaling and filling her with his thick shaft.

"Oh, yes. Fuck me! Fuck me harder! Oh, yes! Yes! Please, faster!"

Abigail shifted so she could lay back, putting one foot on the back of the couch and leaving the other one on the floor. She plunged two fingers into her drenched pussy, fucking it as she imagined Remi's cock taking her. In her fantasy, Gray's fingers went to her nipples, where he pinched and plucked the taut peaks.

"Oh, God, yes! I love that! More, please!" Staring up into Master Gray's eyes, she told him, "Your cock is beautiful. It feels amazing. I can't wait for you to fuck me, too."

A sexy, evil grin spread across his handsome face. "Why should you wait? Open that pretty mouth of yours and take me."

"Yes, Sir."

He fucked her mouth while Remi fucked her cunt. Faster and harder with every thrust until she couldn't hold back the tidal wave of pleasure that flooded her. "*Ohhhh*! Gray! Remi! Yessss! *Ahhhh!*"

She came hard and the men did too. It was pure ecstasy to be taken by both of them at once.

Her eyes slammed shut, as from head to toe, she quaked

from the intense pleasure. When the fireworks behind her eyelids began to fade, Abigail realized she'd been talking out loud during her fantasy, but between the two locked doors, no one could have heard her. Pulling her fingers from her core, she glanced at the ornate clock on a shelf in the dark wood bookcase. Ten minutes before she had to get back to work. As much as she wanted to languish in the afterglow of her orgasm, she stood and pulled down her skirt with one hand. Thankfully, both CEOs had wet bars in their offices, and she stepped over to the sink. After cleaning up as quickly as she could, Abigail wiped down the couch with a damp paper towel, grabbed her e-reader, and took one last look around. Sure there was no sign she'd been there, nor what she'd done, she opened the door and headed to her desk.

CHAPTER THREE

Gray's chauffeur, Byron Glover, pulled up to the main entrance of the building that housed the headquarters of BDR. Before the man could get out of the driver's seat, his boss opened the rear passenger door and climbed out. Gray preferred to do some things for himself, instead of being catered to, with a few exceptions. If he was in a limo going to a big event, he'd let the chauffeur do the grand revealing of who was in the back of the stretch for the paparazzi and fans. And while he drove himself to and from work, it was easier to let Byron drive him to meetings around the city or to the airport rather than having to deal with finding a parking spot most days.

Over the roof of the car, he nodded at the retired police officer who'd taken the job of driving Gray around instead of driving his wife nuts being home with nothing to do. "Thanks, Byron. The rest of the day is yours—my other two meetings are just up the Riverwalk. I'll see you tomorrow."

"Thank you, sir. Miss Turner has me scheduled to pick you up at 11:00 for your luncheon in St. Petersburg. I'll see you then."

Striding toward the front entrance of the forty-two story building, Gray thanked the doorman who held the glass door open for him. Black Diamond Records occupied floors 15 through 24, with the executive offices being on the 21st. He hadn't planned on returning to the office until after four this afternoon, but his luncheon with one of their newer artists and the Englishman's manager had to be rescheduled for another day. The singer had received a phone call about his mother being rushed to the hospital in London for chest pains, and had hightailed it to the airport to fly home. Gray would have Abby send a flower arrangement or something to the hospital. She always seemed to know exactly what was appropriate for any given occasion. Gray had fielded several calls over the past few months with people telling him a lot of thought must have gone into whatever was sent.

Gray was now unexpectedly free until his next meeting which was scheduled at 1:30. Glancing at his watch as he stepped onto the elevator, he decided against calling Remi. His brother had a full day scheduled too, and he'd catch up with him later. With several new or established artists releasing albums soon, a huge fundraiser BDR backed every January for wounded veterans, and a nationwide singing competition they were sponsoring in February, the twins would be busy for the next several weeks. Add onto that list two red carpet events, one in Vegas and the other in New York, and Gray was looking forward to next week's celebration at The Covenant. At least there, he didn't have anyone pitching him artists who couldn't sing, or investments they wanted him to make, or favors they needed. At the club, he could be himself . . . Master Grayson. The only requests he got there were from the submissives asking to scene with him and Remi. All they wanted from the brothers was their dominance and some orgasms, nothing more.

After letting several people exit the elevator, he boarded with two men and one woman, all of whom got off on different floors before he reached the 21st floor. He'd check in with Abby and then ask her to have the restaurant on the top floor send down something for his lunch. Liz must have given her a list of Gray and Remi's food preferences because whenever either woman had ordered lunch for them, there was never anything that they didn't care for in the takeout bag. While Liz had been a fantastic personal secretary, Abby was something more. Gray looked forward to seeing her every day—she brightened up the office with just a smile even though her nervousness around her bosses was evident. He took pleasure in checking in with her from the road or other cities just to hear her voice. Damn, he had to get over this lovesick puppy routine when it came to her. Abby was, and always would be, off limits.

Stepping off the elevator, he walked through the large reception area of BDR. The walls were covered with poster-sized photos of their most successful clients and their gold records. Who knew that two brothers who couldn't sing a note on-key or play a single musical instrument would develop the eyes and ears to recognize some of the most talented entertainers on the planet? It had all started back in college when Remi's roommate was in a rock band popular enough to need a manager. While Painted Toenails had never made it past being a favorite bar band for colleges throughout Florida and Georgia, the Mann brothers had discovered other talent they helped get all the way to national and international radio. They'd produced their first Top-40 album before the age of twenty-five, and a year later the talented Morehead sisters, Keisha, Natasha, and Felisha, who performed as Trinity, won a Grammy for Best New Artist or Group.

The young, female receptionist was on the phone, but

gave Gray a brilliant smile as he passed her desk. It was something he'd grown used to in his late teens and early twenties. Women of all ages found the Mann brothers attractive and flirted with them whenever possible. While the twins had both gone through awkward, gangly stages their first two years of high school, all that had changed when they shot up to over six feet tall the summer before their junior year. Working as lifeguards at the local, public pool, they'd developed tans and muscle tone, carving out physiques they'd been jealous over on other teenage boys the year before. Acne disappeared, Remi's braces came off, and suddenly, they had girls calling the house at all hours, driving their parents nuts.

Striding down the hall, Gray chuckled to himself. Who would have thought back then the two skinny tweens they'd been would've ended up being listed in *People* magazine's Sexiest Men of the Year edition a few months ago? Certainly not him. He wasn't egotistical, but he had to admit, his and Remi's good looks had opened more doors for them than expected, giving them the opportunity to grow their business into a booming success.

The outer door to his and Remi's offices was locked. Through the glass, he saw Abby wasn't at her desk and figured she must have gone out to lunch. But, then again, there was a partially-eaten sandwich and a bottle of Diet Coke sitting on her desk. *Hmm. Maybe she's in the ladies' room or something.*

Gray pulled his passkey from his pocket and unlocked and opened the door before letting it close softly behind him again. Both office doors were shut and, unlike the outer one, there were no windows to see into the rooms. Heading for his own office, he skirted Abby's desk and stopped short when he heard her voice coming faintly from Remi's office.

While it was definitely her, the tone of her voice sounded different, unlike anything he'd heard from her before. It sounded husky and breathless, not the timid, stuttering he often found endearing.

His eyes narrowed as he stepped toward the closed door of his brother's office.

"Oh, yes. Fuck me! Fuck me harder! Oh, yes! Yes! Please, faster!"

What the goddamn fuck? Gray saw red as fury raced through his body. Remi's fucking Abby? After we'd agreed she was off limits! The son of a fucking bitch, I'm going to kill him!

Gray reached for the doorknob, intent on breaking up the fuck fest, but he froze. As furious as he was, he couldn't embarrass Abby, and the last thing he'd do was make her the subject of nasty gossip throughout BDR. And the way he felt right now, throwing Remi out the window from the 21st floor was a very good possibility. It would also be impossible to hope no one would notice.

"Oh, God, yes! I love that! More, please! Your cock is beautiful. It feels amazing."

His fists and jaw clenched as he turned on his heel and stormed out of the office, shutting the door behind him before heading toward the elevators. He didn't want to hear Abby as the orgasm hit her when he couldn't watch her come apart in ecstasy. As for Remi, Gray would deal with him when the bastard got home later.

CLIMBING from his Porsche Cayenne Turbo S, Remi grabbed his briefcase and strode toward the front door. It'd been a long day and he was looking forward to a soak in the hot tub and then some sleep. Tomorrow, he and Gray were taking their private jet to Las Vegas for the weekend for the United Country Music Awards being held at Mandalay Bay Resort and Casino. Several of their country music artists were up for big awards and it appeared it would be a great night for BDR.

He'd packed last night, so he was set to head to the private airport they used tomorrow afternoon. Abby had made their morning agendas light, but there was one luncheon meeting they had scheduled for 11:30 with local socialite Katherine Vaughn-Hopkins. The woman was on countless committees for one charity or another, and her new project was a free music school for underprivileged children. Of course, her first phone call to solicit funds and get planning input had been to her best friend's twin sons who'd never been able to turn the older woman down.

Their "aunt" Katherine and mother had become good friends in their twenties when Melinda Mann had been the daytime nurse for the other woman's ailing mother. Katherine's family had come from old money, and instead of putting their matriarch in a nursing facility, they'd brought the medical care to her in the home she loved. While the elderly woman's body had been failing, her mind had still been sharp as a tack and Melinda had gotten to know her very well as she cared for her for over a year, with Katherine visiting every day. Remi's mom said she cried just as hard as Mrs. Vaughn's children when she'd finally passed in her sleep one night. The two younger women remained steadfast friends over the years, despite the difference in their social statuses. In fact, Aunt Katherine had been the one who'd backed the twins financially when they were first getting BDR off the ground. It was why they could never say no to any favor she called them about.

Opening the door, Remi walked in and never had a

chance to evade the fist that came flying, hitting him square in the face. His lower jaw felt like it had exploded into a million pieces as he stumbled back out the door and onto his ass. As he quickly got to his feet again, the only other thing besides the pain that registered in his mind was his assailant was Grayson, and he was beyond pissed about something. "What the fuck, Gray?"

"You son of a fucking bitch!"

This time, Remi saw the punch coming and was able to duck then tackle his brother back into the house, landing hard on the granite tile in the foyer. They both barely missed cracking their heads on a heavy, round, wooden table with a huge silk flower arrangement on it, courtesy of an interior decorator. It'd been a long time since the two had come to blows over something, but it did happen once in a while—however, usually Remi knew in advance why they were punching the shit out of each other.

Even though Gray was an inch taller and fifteen pounds heavier than him, they were still evenly matched. Fists, elbows, and knees made contact as they rolled across the floor. Grunts and curses filled the air. Remi managed to get the upper hand, but not for long as Gray used his leg to throw his brother off him.

"You couldn't leave her alone, could you?" Gray spat. "You had to go and fuck her!"

Breathing heavily, they both rolled to their feet and stood, and Remi ducked another punch. "What the fuck are you talking about? I haven't fucked anyone since Aurora! And you were fucking with me!"

"Bullshit! You were fucking Abby in your office this afternoon!"

Remi dodged another fist, grabbed the banister to the stairs, and swung himself up a few steps, out of this brother's reach. "Gray!" His twin froze at the deep, commanding tone

Remi used while sceneing with a sub. Their angry gazes met, and he lowered the volume of his voice. His open hands were up and out to the sides in a "calm the fuck down" gesture. "I have no fucking clue what you're talking about. I left the office at 10:00 and never went back. Didn't you check my schedule? I was in Orlando all day and just got back. I didn't even stop at the office on my way here. Now, what the hell are you talking about? What makes you think I was fucking Abby?"

Wiping the smear of blood from his lip, Gray brought his breathing under control before answering. "If it wasn't you, then our pretty, little secretary was using your office for some afternoon delight with someone. My lunch meeting was cancelled so I went back to the office. The outer door was locked, and when I went in, your door was shut, and Miss Turner was quite vocal about the cock she was getting behind it."

"What?" Remi's bruised jaw dropped. "Are you fucking kidding me?" His brother rolled his eyes. "All right, you're not kidding."

The rage that was written all over Gray's face was now coursing through Remi's veins. Descending the stairs, he strode past his brother and grabbed his briefcase from where it'd landed on the front steps. Shutting the front door, he headed toward the home office with Gray on his heels. "Where are you going?"

Plopping down in the leather, executive desk chair, Remi booted up the computer, as Gray stared at him. "I'm bringing up the security feed for my office."

An evil smirk appeared on his brother's face. While the rest of BDR was on the master security system, Remi and Gray hadn't wanted anyone to have access to what happened behind their office doors. That was why they'd had Brody Evans from Trident Security set them up with an alternate system for the two rooms, just in case it was ever needed. Evans and the Mann brothers were the only ones with access, and they trusted Ian Sawyer's employee, and their fellow Dom at The Covenant, not to view the feeds unless it was necessary.

As Remi brought up the recording, complete with audio, for his office from earlier in the day, Gray rounded the desk and stood behind him. "If it's Crawford, we're firing his ass."

"If it's any employee of BDR, we're firing his ass, after we kick it. What time did you say?"

"About 12:30, give or take a few."

Remi stopped the recording at 12:15 then did a slow fast forward until they saw the door to his empty office open. He hit a button and it returned to normal speed as Abby stepped inside—alone—and shut the door. *Huh?*

The two brothers watched dumbfounded as their sweet, innocent secretary hiked up her skirt and sat down on the leather couch. One hand was holding an e-reader, while the other dropped between her spread legs and pushed her white panties aside. Remi's sore jaw nearly hit the floor. "Holy shit! Are you seeing this?"

Gray didn't answer the rhetorical question, he just leaned on the back of the chair Remi was sitting in.

Abby's hand rubbed her clit and pussy, and it was only a few moments until she put aside whatever she'd been reading on the digital device. Her husky voice came through loud and clear. "Yes, Master Remi, I'm so naughty. I need to be punished for losing that important file you needed."

Remi's brows shot up as he felt Gray stiffen behind him at the mention of his name—and title—but he couldn't tear his gaze away from Abby to question his brother. She was obviously responding to a fantasy playing out in her head as her hand moved faster and faster.

"T-ten, Sir?"

Her eyes fluttered shut and her hips bucked. "*Ohhhh.* Yes, Sirs. Spank me. Please, spank me so I don't forget next time."

"Sirs?" Gray sounded as shocked as Remi felt. Holy shit, their innocent secretary was not so innocent. Who would've guessed?

Her hips flexed a few more times and Remi's cock hardened almost to the point of pain. "Oh, yes. Fuck me! Fuck me harder! Oh, yes! Yes! Please, faster!"

Gray slapped Remi's shoulder. "That's what I heard! I almost busted the door down."

"I'm surprised you didn't," he muttered, his eyes still glued to the computer monitor.

Abby shifted so she could lay down and put one foot up on the back of the couch. Now they had a perfect view of her pussy and could even tell how wet she was. Her fingers plunged inside as she fucked herself and, damn, he was going to cum just watching her get herself off. "Oh, God, yes! I love that! More, please! Your cock is beautiful. It feels amazing. I can't wait for you to fuck me, too."

Too? Holy shit, she's fantasizing about us topping her together!

"*Ohhhh*! Gray! Remi! *Yessss! Ahhhhh*!"

Behind him, Gray inhaled sharply. Yup, big-brother-by-one-minute was in serious need of relief, too. They watched in rapt attention as Abby shattered in ecstasy, and it was the most beautiful thing Remi had ever seen. After coming back down to earth, Abby had cleaned up and then left the room. Remi swiveled the chair so he could see his twin's face, which showed a combination of astonishment and lust.

Gray's gaze met his. "I think we need to reconsider our self-imposed, no-touch policy about our little secretary, don't you?"

In the past, they'd talked about finding a woman to permanently share their lives with. Someone who'd not only be their submissive, but their wife. They'd just been biding their time until the right woman came along. And now it seemed as though the right woman had been under their noses all along—at least, for the last six months. "Fuck, yeah! I was hoping you'd say that!"

CHAPTER FOUR

"Abby, can you come in here, please?"

"Yes, sir." Abigail grabbed the pad and pen she used to jot down notes so she wouldn't forget anything and hurried into Remi's office. Instead of sitting behind his desk, the man was perched on his leather couch . . . in the exact same spot she'd been in the day before, masturbating. Trying to push the memory from her mind, her cheeks turned pink as she stood before him. "What do you need, sir?"

Remi sat back and spread his arms over the back of the couch. One leg came up and he rested the ankle on the opposite knee. God, he was gorgeous. No matter what he wore, he could grace the cover of a magazine and have women drooling over him. Today, he was wearing brown loafers, khaki pants, and a tucked in, long-sleeved, white Henley with the top two buttons undone. A smattering of fine chest hair teased her through the V. He'd gotten a haircut sometime between when she'd seen him yesterday and this morning. And something else about him was different. There was a bruise on his left jawline, barely noticeable under the coarse stubble. He hadn't shaved this morning—maybe to hide the discoloration? *What happened?* "There's been some changes in our schedules over the next few days you need to be aware of."

The door behind her closing caught her attention, and glancing over her shoulder, she found Gray had entered the room. He strode over and sat in a wingback chair catty-corner to the couch. "Good morning, Abby." His deep, sexy voice rumbled through her, and she felt it all the way to her toes.

"G-Good morning, s-sir." Damn, why couldn't she stop stuttering around these two men? Gray was dressed just as casually as his brother, but his black jeans were topped off with a sky blue polo with the BDR logo on it. He'd also gotten a haircut, but that wasn't so unusual since the two had the music awards to go to this weekend in Vegas. She also didn't miss his swollen and split lower lip. *Had they been in an accident?* No—as their personal secretary, she'd have been fending off calls from the paparazzi if that had happened. *A fight?* Again, the press would have been all over that if there'd been a hint the Mann brothers had been in a bar brawl somewhere—not that it had ever happened before, to her knowledge. So, what the hell *had* happened?

As he got comfortable in the chair, Gray raised a disapproving eyebrow at her. "Abby, I've asked you repeatedly to call me by my first name here at the office, when clients aren't around, and so has Remi. What do we need to do to remind you of that, hmm? A spanking, perhaps?" His right hand subtly twitched where it lay on the arm of the chair, as if that was exactly what he wanted to do.

Her eyes grew the size of saucers and her mouth fell open. *Holy shit*! Was he fucking kidding? No . . . nope . . . he definitely was not kidding. Not with that hard, commanding look on his face. Had she missed a memo that the office was going to be in an alternate universe today—where her fantasies could come true? That was the only explanation she could think of for his questions. "Um . . . n-no, s-sir, I mean, Gray. I-I'm sorry, it's just . . . um . . . a hard habit t-to break, sir—Gray!"

Silence permeated the room, broken only by the ticking of the clock in the bookcase, and the walls seemed to close in as the two men stared at her. Abigail couldn't help squirming where she stood, looking back and forth between them in confusion and arousal. Finally, her gaze settled on Remi. "Um . . . sir . . . I mean, Remi, you s-said something about . . ." She swallowed the lump in her throat. " . . . about a few schedule changes?"

A lazy grin spread across his handsome face, bringing out his adorable dimples. Abigail suddenly felt like she was in a lion's den, and she was the beast's next meal. Remi gently patted the couch next to him. "Please sit, and we'll go over everything."

Her heart threatened to beat out of her chest as she took one then two tentative steps toward the couch. Pivoting, she slowly lowered herself to the soft leather, her back ramrod straight, doing her best to not appear obvious in her attempt to sit as far away from Remi as possible. She put a shaking pen tip to the top page of her pad. "O-okay. I'm ready."

"Are you, now?"

Her gaze shot to Gray. Those three innocent words had sounded as if they'd been saturated in sex and sin. She felt a flush of wetness coat her panties and clenched her thighs together. "Y-yes, s—Gray."

A near duplicate of his brother's smile appeared. "Very good, Abby. You're finally learning. I should threaten to spank you more often." Without pause, and ignoring the stunned look on her face, he continued in his normal, business voice. "As Remi stated, plans have changed. I spoke to Katherine Hopkins and told her you'd be contacting her next week to reschedule today's luncheon." Abigail began writing, using the shorthand she'd learned long ago. "The next thing you need to do is arrange for someone to fill in for you for the rest of today and all of Monday. As soon as we're done with this little meeting, you'll have two hours to go home and pack, then Byron will pick you up to take you to the airport. You'll be going to Vegas with us."

The pen flew out of Abigail's hand into Remi's lap. He glanced down, and the amusement in his eyes was evident as he picked up the pen and handed it back to her. "Problem, little one?"

"Uh . . . Vegas? W-Why am I going to Vegas?" It wasn't that she'd never travelled with them for business before—Liz had too—just never for an entire weekend for an awards ceremony.

"Because we have a seat between us that needs to be filled at the awards, and we'd like you to be the one filling it." After finding out Aurora had been cheating on them, it was no wonder they didn't want her near them at the United Country Music Awards. But that didn't explain why they wanted Abigail to fill the spot. There were plenty of women who'd love to be sandwiched between the two gorgeous men and hob-knobbing it with celebrities, to boot. "Do you have a gown to wear?"

She knew Gray and Remi would be wearing their custom-fit, designer tuxedos to the event, and to her dismay, there was nothing in her closet that came close to being red-carpet worthy. Her clothes were more like drab, gray-carpet worthy. "Um . . . no, I don't. Why don't you take someone else? I'm s-sure there are plenty of woman who'd love to attend it with you." She inwardly cursed the wave of jealousy that came over her at the thought of them taking another woman to the ceremony.

Remi reached over and took her hand in his, rubbing his

thumb over the back of it. Electric warmth shot through her, pushing aside the green-eyed monster. His voice dropped until it was as smooth as the fine whiskey she knew he favored. "Because we don't want to take anyone else. Don't worry about something to wear. I'm sure you'll be able to find something in one of the many shops in Vegas. Our treat."

Mesmerized by the small circular motions his thumb was making on her skin, she almost missed what he'd said. "I-I can't ask you to buy me a dress to wear. Seriously, you should ask someone else to go with you."

Gray stood and approached her. Before she realized his intent, he bent down and put one arm under her knees and the other behind her back, then lifted. She squeaked at suddenly being airborne and dropped her pad and pen to grab his shoulders, but he ignored her response as he took her place on the couch and settled her on his lap. Abigail froze in his arms. He cupped her chin and turned her head until she was looking into his eyes. "Little one, I don't think you understand. You *will* be going to Vegas with us, and you *will* let us buy you a dress worthy of your beauty, and you *will* be attending the award ceremony on our arms. End of story."

AFTER THE PRIVATE jet leveled off at cruising altitude, Remi stood and walked back to the small kitchen. Usually they had a flight attendant onboard, but this time the twins wanted privacy, so with a quick phone call this morning, they'd arranged for lunch to be left for them. No one else was on the plane except for the pilot and co-pilot.

Gray studied her, sitting in one of the plush, luxury chairs, with the seatbelt still across her lap. Her nervousness was apparent, but at least she'd followed his order that she change into comfortable, casual clothes for the flight. No longer in one of her prim and proper business suits, she now wore a black, pleated, wool skirt, which came to her knees, over black leggings, a light-weight, short-sleeved, pink sweater that hugged her enticing curves, and cute ankle boots. Her golden brown hair was down from the severe bun she normally wore to work, and he decided then and there he was banning her from wearing it up in the office. He wanted to be able to wrap the long strands around his arm any time he wanted to. Hopefully, by the time they got home from Vegas on Monday afternoon, they'd have a contract in place, giving him and Remi the right to touch her any way they wanted, when they wanted. And she'd no longer be allowed to wear leggings under her skirts, unless it was for warmth. Hell, she wouldn't be allowed to wear anything under her skirts. He liked quick and easy access. How they'd both written off her natural submissiveness as innocence was beyond him, but now as he eyed her, he saw the sex kitten she hid just under the surface, where she probably hoped no one would notice.

Standing, he closed the distance between them and reached down to unclick her seatbelt. When he noticed she was wide-eyed and holding her breath at his near and looming proximity, he caressed her soft cheek with the back of his fingers. "Relax, little one. You're safe with us."

She gulped. "I-I know that, s—Gray."

A chuckle escaped him along with a smile. She really was trying to break her habit and that pleased him more than he'd expected. At least when they started to play with her, it would be second nature for her to call them Sir.

Her jaw dropped when he went to his knees in front of her and picked up her right foot, removing her boot. He winked at her as he dug his thumbs into her arch. "It's a long flight, so you might as well be comfortable. Lean back and close your eyes. Let us take care of you." When she hesitated, he lowered his voice to his commanding Dom tone. "That wasn't a request, Abby. Close your eyes and relax."

"Um . . . okay."

While her eyelids fell, the rest of her remained rigid. He'd keep massaging her feet until she finally relaxed if it took him the entire flight. Remi returned from the back with a tray of assorted food which he placed on a table next to the couch. He grinned at the sight of Gray on his knees, but didn't say a word as he walked to the back again and brought out an open bottle of Riesling and three wine glasses. When they clinked in his hand, Abigail's eyes flew open. Letting go of her foot, Gray stood and retrieved the small carry-on duffel he'd brought with him. It was one of his toy bags. Opening the zipper, he quickly located the item he wanted and closed the bag again. He didn't want Abigail to see what else was in there until she was ready.

Striding back to her, he showed her what was in his hand as Remi poured the wine. "This is a blindfold, little one. Since you can't keep your eyes closed as I ordered, you'll wear this."

He did his best not to laugh at the stunned look on her face. Stretching the strap of the blindfold, he slipped it over her head and settled it into place. "Comfy?"

"I-I guess, but . . ."

"But what, sweetheart?"

She swallowed. "I just don't understand what . . . why . . . I'm sorry, I'm confused about all this."

Remi lifted her hand and placed a half-filled glass in it. "Take a sip and we'll explain." Again, she hesitated, but then followed his instructions. "Do you like it? It's a Domaine de la Romanée-Conti. One of my favorite wines."

"It's delicious."

As she took another sip, Gray went back down on his knees and removed her other boot. His thumbs went straight to her arch and began to massage it. "Are you happy working for us, Abby?"

"Y-Yes! Did I do something that made you think I don't like working for you?"

Hmm. They'd have to work on her insecurity. "Not at all. In fact, we think you're the best secretary we've ever had. It just occurred to us we never told you that—never showed you how much we appreciate you. It's time that changed."

"Uh . . . thank you. I love working for you, too."

"Glad to hear it." Remi brought a strawberry to her mouth. "Open your mouth and take a bite, sweetheart."

Almost daily, she enjoyed berries, melons, and grapes as a morning or afternoon snack at her desk. Gray remembered every little detail about her she showed them at work. Now, he was looking forward to learning other details that weren't exactly appropriate at work—like what she sounded like and looked like in the throes of passion that wasn't self-induced.

Remi waited patiently for her to follow his command. When she parted her pretty lips, he rubbed the sweet fruit along her bottom lip. Her tongue peeked out to take a taste, and Gray held back a groan as he felt himself harden. Opening her mouth wider, she let his twin place the strawberry between her teeth before she bit down. As she chewed, her tongue swiped across her lips, catching the red juices coating them. It took everything in Gray not to pull her toward him and kiss her. That would have to wait a little longer, and he'd be damned if he couldn't look into her eyes when she realized the kiss was coming.

Sitting on the couch next to her, Remi took her empty hand in his. He began to massage her palm and fingers like Gray was doing to her foot. "Take another sip of wine, Abby."

"Are you trying to get me drunk?"

His frown quickly became a grin when he realized she was teasing him. Her body was also relaxing under their ministrations—her chin tipped up until her head hit the back of the couch, and her shoulders sagged. It appeared when they took away her sight, and let her other senses take over, her nervousness ebbed. She was giving in to their control just as they'd hoped—exactly as a natural submissive should. They could build on this—the seduction of sweet Abby had begun.

He nodded at Gray, who took the lead as his hands moved to her calves, continuing to caress her. "Abby, Remi and I want to talk to you about something. You know we prefer to date the same woman at the same time, correct? It's not like we've hid it from you or anyone else."

"Yes. I-I know that."

"Have you ever thought about being loved by two men at once? About them taking care of you in every possible way? And before you open that pretty, little mouth, I should warn you we want the truth. There's nothing to be embarrassed about, but neither one of us will tolerate being lied to. Now, answer my question. Have you ever fantasized about two men pleasuring you at the same time?"

Her mouth opened and closed several times. This was a huge struggle for her, they knew, but unless she admitted it to them and herself, she would be resistant to their advances. Gray kneaded her calf muscles as Remi brought her hand to his lips and sucked her index finger into his mouth. Abigail gasped and her hips began to squirm. Gray knew if he ran his hands up her legs, he'd find her pussy hot and wet. "Answer me, little one."

"Uh . . ." Remi licked the V between her first two fingers. Abigail's pelvis bucked forward and she gasped as if it had been her pussy that had been tongued. "Oh, God! Yes!" Her face flushed with a combination of embarrassment and desire. "I mean . . . oh . . . I'm . . ."

"*Shh,* sweetheart. That's exactly what we wanted to hear."

"W-Why?"

"Because Remi and I have been fantasizing about you for months now. And since we're fantasizing about you, and you're fantasizing about two men pleasing you, it's about time we did something about it. We want you, Abby. We're going to seduce you. Please you. Care for you. We plan to make you ours. But before you say yes . . . or no . . . there are some things you need to learn about us, about what we want to do with you . . . and to you." They had no idea if she was aware they were Dominants in the lifestyle or if she'd just been fantasizing about some slap and tickle when she'd been getting herself off in Remi's office. They'd have to take this slowly. She now knew they wanted her, but she had no idea what that entailed. It was time for her to learn. His hands had worked their way up to her thighs, just under her skirt, and he squeezed them gently. "Will you give us a chance?"

"Um . . . w-why me?"

Remi's eyes narrowed. "What do you mean, why you?"

"Y-You could have any woman in the world. Why me? I mean, I'm definitely not Aurora."

"Thank God for that," Gray muttered loud enough for her to hear.

"I mean, I'm not tall, skinny, and blonde."

Remi frowned, clearly not happy she thought she couldn't compete with Aurora Locke—Gray didn't like it either. In fact, in any competition, Abby would win first place every time.

"We know that, Abby," his younger twin said. "We also know you're one of the most beautiful women we've ever met. Women come in all shapes and sizes—that doesn't matter to us. What matters is how that woman makes us feel and how we make her feel." He took her hand and put it on his groin, gently holding it there. Beneath the blindfold, her brow shot up. "This is how you make me feel, little one. And

I guarantee my brother is just as hard, wanting you. But we're going to take this slowly. As Gray said, we're going to seduce you and educate you. And when the time comes, if we're meant to be, you'll submit to our every whim, and we'll show you how beautiful you are to us."

"Do you want that, Abby?" Gray asked, resisting the urge to let his hands go any further up her thighs. If they did, he'd give into the desire to shred the leggings from her body.

"I . . . I'm . . . uh . . . I'm scared."

"Nothing to be scared of, sweetheart. For now, just know that we're interested in getting to know you much, much better, and we plan on seducing you. That means we'll be touching you. Kissing you. Whispering in your ear how we feel about you. And when you're ready, we'll be making love to you . . . at the same time. If you want to try this with us, say 'yes, Sir.'"

Leaning forward, Remi put his mouth to her ear, "Please, trust us, little one. Let us show you how beautiful you are to us. Let us make all your fantasies come true."

After a shiver coursed through her, Abigail took a deep breath and let it out slowly. "I must be crazy . . . or-or dreaming or something, but yes, Sir . . . Sirs."

CHAPTER FIVE

In a daze, Abigail followed Remi and the bellhop to the private elevator that would take them to the sky suite they'd be staying in. Gray walked beside her and his hand rested at her lower back. The heat from his palm penetrated her sweater and her skin, sending bolts of electricity through her.

The Aria Resort & Casino was gorgeous. A chauffeured limousine had been waiting for the trio at the airport, and when they arrived at the hotel, they were brought to a private entrance and check-in, away from the regular front desk. Even if Abigail hadn't known the brothers preferred to stay here whenever they traveled to Vegas—she was, of course, in charge of booking the suite for them—she'd know by the way the staff interacted with them. They were both addressed as Mr. Mann or sir and welcomed with the familiarity of well-liked and frequent guests. Remi had even inquired about the check-in manager's new grandchild, which had caused the older woman to beam with pride as she'd answered him.

When the elevator door opened, the bellhop pushed the

laden luggage cart to the back of the car, then held the doors open for the guests to board. As the twins escorted her, Remi on her left, Gray on her right, the bellhop inserted a key into a panel and then pressed the button for the top floor. Her bosses stood so close to her, towering over her, that Abigail should have felt claustrophobic. Instead, her pounding heart had nothing to do with a fear of being in a closed space, and everything to the sudden change in their attitudes and attention toward her. With her hand at her side, she subtly pinched the outside of her thigh for at least the tenth time since they'd taken her blindfold off a few hours ago.

Remi leaned down and whispered, "Stop pinching yourself, little one. Unless it turns you on. In that case, I'll be more than happy to do it for you. But I should warn you, my fingers would prefer to pinch your delectable ass."

Okay, maybe it hadn't been so subtle. Her eyes shot toward the bellhop. If he'd overheard Remi, he didn't show it. Glancing up, she saw a teasing smirk on Remi's handsome face. *Abby, meet Alice and the rest of the characters in the rabbit hole,* she thought to herself. There was no way this was real. She had to be dreaming and would wake up in a few hours, in time for work.

The door slid open and Abigail's jaw dropped as she stepped directly into an elegant foyer. The few times she'd traveled with one CEO or the other for business, she'd stayed in a regular hotel room by herself. They'd always been five-star rooms, but there'd been nothing more than a bed, bathroom, and small sitting area in them. This was like walking into a 2400 square foot, mini mansion. The suite included a gourmet kitchen, dining room with a five-stool bar, and a huge living room overlooking a private pool and the Vegas strip. A gold-toned circular staircase went up to the second floor where she assumed the bedrooms were located.

"Sirs, it's nice to see you again. Welcome back to the Aria." Abigail turned to see a tall, thin, gray-haired man in an impeccable, black suit. He smiled and bowed his head slightly at her. "Good afternoon, miss, my name is Fergus, and I'll be your daytime butler. If you need anything at all, I'll take care of it at once."

"T-Thank you."

Remi put his arm around her waist and tucked her close, sending a warm flush throughout her body. "Fergus, this is Abigail Turner. Whatever she wants, she gets. There's no need to seek our approval."

"As you wish, sir. It's a pleasure to meet you, Ms. Turner. Is there anything I can get for you right now?"

Both brothers looked at her expectantly, and she still had that rabbit hole feeling. Shaking her head, she replied, "No, thank you. And it's nice to meet you, too."

"Thank you, miss." Fergus pointed to a small box on the wall next to the elevator. "The intercoms are located in each room, and I can be summoned by pushing the red button. If there's nothing you need at the moment, I'll see to your suitcases."

Abigail realized the bellhop hadn't gotten off the elevator with them. He must have taken it to the upper floor with their bags.

A cell phone rang and Remi pulled his out of his pocket, glancing at the number. He nodded at Gray, then turned around and walked toward the dining room, answering the phone as he went. Abigail took in her surroundings and stepped over to the floor-to-ceiling windows. Dark, heavy clouds were blocking the sun, but with the myriad of neon lights of the strip, she'd never know it.

She jumped when hands closed around her waist and Gray whispered in her ear, "First time in Vegas, little one? It can be a bit overwhelming."

"Yes, it is. But it's beautiful, too." It was disconcerting having him this close, especially when all she wanted to do was lean back against his hard chest. His warm breath against her skin as he spoke had her clenching her thighs together. After they'd set her head spinning and her blood boiling on the jet, they'd backed off and allowed her to remove the blindfold. Things had then returned to normal . . . well, not exactly normal. They'd begun asking her questions about her likes and dislikes, about her family and friends—stuff that was usually discussed on a first date. But Abigail had never had a first date anywhere close to that. Crap, she shouldn't even call it a date. It was her bosses getting to know her better . . . after they'd told her they were going to seduce her. *Holy hell.*

"We're going to skip tonight's parties; there'll be plenty tomorrow and Sunday night to attend. We're going to take you out on the town. We'll start with an early dinner at Joel Robuchon's, then a trip over to Fremont Street, which you'll love, and after that, we have front row tickets for one of the Cirque du Soleil shows. Sound good?"

It sounded amazing. Not the dinner or the trip to Fremont Street, whatever that was, or the show. No, what sounded amazing was she would be spending hours with the two handsomest men on the planet and there was nothing work related about it. She hoped the dress she'd brought with her was appropriate enough for the evening.

Abigail loved how Gray's hands stayed on her waist as she turned around to face him. Tilting her head back, her gaze met his. The heat she saw in those hazel eyes seared her soul. "It-It . . . um . . . sounds wonderful."

Bending down, Gray stopped his mouth a scant inch or two from hers. "I'm going to kiss you, sweet Abby, because I can't resist the temptation anymore. If you don't want me to, tell me now."

Her eyes went wide. *Tell him no?* Yeah, that was so not going to happen. This might be her only chance to kiss Grayson Mann, and she'd be crazy not to. Actually, it was crazy to kiss him. How could she go back to work for the twins on Monday after they realized they weren't really attracted to her? This had to be a fling for them—she was just one of the many women who they'd shared before moving on.

But none of that mattered as Gray closed the last bit of distance between them. She'd waited too long without saying no, and now it was too late. His lips brushed against hers, and she forgot why she'd wanted to say no in the first place. Hell, she'd even forgotten her own name!

Her lips tingled, and his made another gentle pass over them. Abigail's eyes fluttered shut as Gray nibbled on her bottom lip. His tongue swiped a taste of her as he took a step forward, backing her up against the window. His hands cupped her jaw and . . .

"Ahem. Started without me, huh?"

Abigail jumped at the sound of Remi's voice, and her face flushed in a combination of embarrassment and lust. Gray lifted his head, but his gaze remained on her as he smiled. "Sorry, brother. You were taking too long. Are we all set?"

"Yup. 11:00 a.m. tomorrow." Remi came toward them as Gray turned her around in his arms to face his brother. He pulled her against his length and she could feel his impressive hard-on at her lower back. Remi stopped in front of her and cupped her jaw as Gray had done moments before. "You're right. I was taking too long and think it's time to remedy that."

As Gray ran his hands up and down her shoulders, arms, and sides, Remi bent his head and kissed her. His lips were a combination of soft and hard, and he took possession of her mouth without hesitation. Not as gentle as Gray had been, but Abigail didn't mind. Hell, no, she didn't mind at all. The man could kiss. His tongue probed her lips, urging her to open for him. She wasn't exactly inexperienced—she wasn't a virgin—and had dated occasionally over her twenty-nine years on Earth. A few suitors had even lasted several months. But compared to Gray and Remi, those had been immature boys. These two were men. Men who could teach her so much. Men who could break her heart in an instant.

Involuntarily, her body stiffened at that thought, and Remi lifted his head, staring into her eyes. "Something wrong, little one? A little too fast?"

All she could do was nod in response and both men backed off. *Both men* . . . holy crap, she'd kissed both within a matter of seconds, and neither of them minded. They weren't jealous of each other, that was clear. But Abigail had this feeling of dread . . . and shame. A feeling of being a slut. "I-I'm sorry . . . I'm not what you want. I'm not sure I can do this."

Gray came around and stood next to his brother. Neither one seemed mad, more like concerned. Gray slid his hands into the pocket of his pants. "Can't do what, Abby? Can't love two men at once? Can't let two men love you at the same time? We understand it's not the norm of society, but that doesn't make it wrong. We won't force you into anything, but we'd like you to read some articles on a website to help you decide once and for all if you can try this. As for what we want, all we want is to pamper you, pleasure you, and be with you. Everything else is negotiable."

"Do you know what Dominants and submissives are, little one?" Remi asked as Gray strode over to a long, narrow desk that doubled as a table behind one of the couches. A computer was there for their use, and he began to boot it up.

Holy shit! "Um . . . y-yes. I-I'm reading a book right now a-about that . . . um . . . lifestyle. Are you . . . are you saying you're . . . um . . ."

Remi raised an eyebrow and ignored the second question she hadn't been able to complete. "Book? What book would that be?"

"Um . . . it's fiction. You know, a romance/suspense novel. It's called *Velvet Vixen*, by Kristen Anders." Pink spread across her cheeks. What had made her admit she was reading a smut book? Actually it was more of a classy smut book—Kristen Anders was a popular writer in the BDSM genre, and Abigail had loved the three books she'd written on the lifestyle as well as her vanilla romances.

"Ah, Kristen's books are excellent, from what I hear—she keeps them as real as possible, encouraging safe, sane, and consensual practices. However, I'm more of a CIA or political thriller fan, so I haven't read them. She's actually married to a friend of ours. I'll have to let her know you enjoy her books. You do enjoy them, right? I mean, you wouldn't be reading them if you didn't enjoy them."

"You know Kristen Anders? Wow . . . um . . . yes, I do enjoy them. I'm actually 'friends' . . ." She made air quotes with her fingers. " . . . with her on Facebook. I'm friends with a lot of authors and other readers on there. It's a huge community, of sorts. It's so nice how she interacts with her readers. One of these days, I'll get to one of her book signings and finally meet her." A wide grin appeared on Remi's face and his eyes danced in amusement. "Wh-what?"

He shrugged a shoulder. "I'll take care of introducing her to you, soon. And I've noticed that when you talk about something you love or are passionate about, you seem to forget your nervousness around Gray and me. You did that on the plane, too, when you were talking about your dads."

Her dads. Abigail's fathers were a gay couple who'd been together for thirty-two years, but had only been able to legally marry last year after same-sex marriage was allowed in Florida. She'd been born by surrogate—a fact she'd never been ashamed of. She loved her Pa and Dad, Percy and Steven Turner, respectively, and always supported them as they'd supported her—with all their hearts. Percy was a radiologist, while Steven was a pharmacist in the same St. Petersburg hospital as his husband. She'd been glad to see neither Gray nor Remi appeared to be bothered by the fact she had two fathers.

"Come here, Abby." She went to where Gray was holding the desk chair out for her. "We have about an hour or so before we have to get ready for dinner, so I want you to use that time to read the Q&A page of this website. You can also go into the chat rooms as they are very receptive to questions from newbies."

She slowly lowered herself into the chair as she stared at the computer screen. "*BDSM 101*? There's really a website for that?"

He chuckled. "There seems to be a website for everything these days. Anyway, this is the one the submissives at our club prefer as the site frowns on creepers joining or anyone giving bad advice. Happy reading."

Kissing her on top of the head, he joined Remi in the sitting area and turned on the TV. Taking a deep but shaky breath, Abigail began to read.

CHAPTER SIX

Worried, Remi paced the living room. If she turned them down, he'd be devastated. Gray would be, too. Abby was her . . . the woman they'd been searching for all their lives. He'd known it deep down in his soul the moment he'd kissed her. Any doubts he may have had up to that point had faded away. Sweet Abby Turner was theirs. Now they just had to convince her of that fact.

She was nervous, scared, unsure, and experiencing every other negative feeling that could have her running from them. At least she hadn't done just that after reading the BDSM website for about forty-five minutes. She'd stood, and when Gray had asked if she had any questions for them, her response had been, "Do you mind if I do some thinking for a little bit? While I get ready for dinner?" Unfortunately, she hadn't looked directly at them, and her cheeks had been a deep pink, so they had no idea what she'd been thinking.

Now, she was still upstairs in the suite's master bedroom —the one with the super king-sized bed. Gray and he had taken the second bedroom with two queen-sized beds, and he hoped like hell before Monday, they'd all be in the king with Abby sleeping between them.

"Stop pacing."

Remi rolled his eyes at his brother, but continued moving back and forth. "I pace when I've got something on my mind—you know this. What if this blows up in our faces? You were right—we could lose her as both our woman and our secretary."

Taking a seat on the couch, Gray adjusted the open collar of his pale, green dress shirt, which he'd paired with black chinos. "We just have to take it slowly. Everything will be fine."

Remi wished he was as confident about this as his twin. "Are we going to tell her about the video?"

"At some point, I think we should—honesty being the best policy and all that. But definitely not until she's signed a contract."

"A contract that's not worth a hill of beans if she decides to walk."

Gray sighed. "Chill, Remi. One thing at a time, all right? Let's get through tonight's question and answer period, and get her more comfortable being close to us."

The sound of the master bedroom door shutting had them both looking up to see Abby coming down the stairs. And holy fucking hell, she was a walking hard-on. Her golden brown hair had been blown out and framed her face in soft waves. Understated makeup made her eyes and lips pop. As she followed the circular staircase down, they were able to see more and more of her. She was wearing a vintage-style dress, circa the 1950s, and it was one of the sexiest things Remi had ever seen. The black, three-quarter-length-sleeved dress had a sweetheart neckline with a narrow piece of black and white, floral trim over her breasts. The same pattern appeared under a slit in the pleated skirt, which fell just below her knees. But it was the cut of the dress that blew him away. It narrowed at her waist and accentuated her womanly curves, giving her a rockin', hour-glass figure. Yup, definitely a walking hard-on. He tried to subtly adjust himself in the tan dress pants he wore with a button-down, black shirt.

As she reached the first floor, Remi's eyes dropped to her feet. *Fuck me!* She'd finished the dress off with sheer, black stockings and red, chunky-heeled shoes which also had a retro style to them. In one hand, she held a red, clutch purse. She paused, eyeing them with uncertainty.

He could see her nervousness was back and wanted to expel it as quickly as possible. "Little one, you look gorgeous. Absolutely stunning, and I, for one, can't wait to show you off to the world. But that also means I'll have to push aside my jealousy of any other man looking at you. With the exception of Gray, of course." The pink he loved to see tinged her cheeks. "Turn all the way around so we can get the whole effect."

She took a half step forward and slowly spun on the ball of her foot. Remi's mouth watered when he saw the sexy seams down the back of the stockings, and planned on finding out later if they were thigh-highs like he suspected. Damn, a woman in thigh-highs was close to number one on his list of the sexiest things in the world.

Gray hadn't said a word yet, and Remi glanced at him. There was unadulterated lust in his brother's eyes as he stood and walked over to Abby. He took her hand and brought it to his lips. "I can't remember the last time I was stunned into silence. Sweetheart, you are exquisite."

Her blush deepened. "Th-thank you."

Sweeping his hand toward the open elevator door waiting for them, Remi said, "Shall we? Because if we don't leave now, I'm going to forget I'm a gentleman and ravage our lovely date."

"I agree," Gray responded. Not letting go of her hand, he led her toward the elevator. Remi followed, his gaze pinned to those sensual seams he couldn't get enough of. The hem of Abby's dress swished from side to side with every step. After all three of them boarded, Gray flipped the hold switch and the doors slid shut.

The brothers stood on either side of Abby. Gray still held her hand, and Remi put his palm at her lower back, using his thumb to caress her. She was a little stiff, still not used to their closeness. As the elevator zoomed to the private lobby, he tried to put her at ease. "Have you ever been to a casino, Abby?"

She nodded. "Yes. My dads like to go every once in a while to the Seminole Hard Rock Casino for a show and some blackjack. I've gone a few times with them, although I'm not a big gambler. I prefer the penny slot machines."

"Have you ever tried craps? I have a feeling you'll be my lucky charm at the table. Maybe we'll test my theory later."

The doors opened, and they headed for the exit where their chauffeured vehicle waited for them. The twins didn't usually use a limo when they were in Vegas. A cab or luxury town car would do, unless they were going to an event like the award show on Sunday. However, they wanted to give Abby the five-star treatment—not to impress her, but because she deserved it. They'd give her the moon if they could.

A uniformed attendant saw them approaching and held the door open for them. Once they were through, a smartly-dressed chauffeur opened the rear door to the black, stretch limo, with a slight bow of his head. "Good evening, sirs, miss. My name is Edward. I understand you're dining at Joel Robuchon's, followed by a trip to Fremont Street, then back to the MGM Grand for a 9:00 show. Have there been any changes to that?"

"No," Remi answered as Gray ducked into the limo first then held his hand out to assist Abby in next to him. "That covers it. After the show, we'll play it by ear."

"Excellent. I'm at your service as long as you need me tonight."

The perks of being a mover and shaker in the entertainment industry were damn good. Climbing in after Abby, Remi settled in as Edward closed the door. He hit a button on a nearby panel that closed the partition between them and the driver. Moments later, the limo pulled away from the curb and out into the evening traffic. Remi's eyes went to Abby's now exposed knees as her dress had ridden up a little. He couldn't resist hooking his finger under the hem and sliding it up a little further.

Abby seemed to panic and slapped her hand down on her thigh, stopping the dress's upward momentum. Her eyes went wide. "I-I'm sorry. I didn't mean to do that."

His gaze softened. "Yes, you did. And I'm the one who should apologize, little one. My curiosity got the best of me. I'm dying to know if you're wearing thigh-highs."

"Why w-would you want to know that?"

A grin spread across his face. From her response and embarrassed expression, he was almost one-hundred percent positive he was right about the stockings. "Because, that would make your outfit even sexier."

"It would?" She didn't seem to believe him, but trusting what he said was the truth would come in time.

"Mm-hmm. But before I go further, I want to make sure you understand a few things. Do you know what a safeword is?" She nodded, and he frowned. "Okay, rule number one, Abby, is we want you to verbalize every answer to our questions. Nodding or shaking your head is not a response;

there's no room for misunderstandings between us. Now, do you know what a safeword is?"

"Yes. It's been in a lot of the books I've read, and it was on the website."

"Explain it to me." She was new to this so it would be a while before she no longer needed encouragement to continue.

"It's . . . um . . . a word that a submissive uses to stop things."

Gray shifted in his seat, probably because he was hard as a rock. He brought his arm up behind Abby's head, along the back of the seat. "If a submissive uses her safeword, then, yes, her Dom will stop the scene or activity. The Dom will also not be angry if the submissive uses her safeword, nor will the submissive be punished in any way for using it."

"But," Remi added. "The submissive should be absolutely certain she wants everything to stop. The club we belong to uses the color system. Red is to stop everything. Yellow is to slow things down until the submissive is comfortable with continuing. Understand?"

She nodded, but quickly realized her mistake. "Yes. Red stops, yellow slows down."

"Okay, now that a safeword has been established. I'd very much like to see if I'm correct that you're wearing thigh-highs. If you want to say your safeword, then I'll understand." He gave her a teasing smile and winked. "I'll die of curiosity, but I'll understand."

He felt her shiver when Gray leaned toward her and nuzzled her ear. "Lift your dress, Abby, and let him take a peek. We can't have Remi dying before we show you what it's like to be pleasured by us at the same time. And don't worry, the driver and anyone outside won't be able to see."

Seconds passed before Abby seemed to make up her mind. Slowly, her fingers gathered up the material of the skirt and pulled it toward her hips. Thigh-highs, just as he'd suspected, and holy hell, he was harder than granite. Abby's eyes were on him as she licked her ruby red lips. An inch at a time, he ran his index finger from her knee upward, giving her time to stop him if things were moving too fast. On her other side, Gray kissed, licked, and nibbled her neck, and she tilted her head to the side, giving him easier access. Her eyes fluttered shut as Remi fingered the top band of the stockings. Her hands clenched the fabric a little tighter, but then she moaned. The sound went straight to his cock, making it twitch with want.

Making small circles with his finger, he went further up her silky, inner thigh. He lowered his voice to his Dom tone. "Spread your legs for me, Abby. Show me how turned on you are right now."

There was only a moment's hesitation before she followed his command. He added his middle finger to the other and found her panties damp and hot—scorching hot. He rubbed her pussy through the material as Gray cupped her breast and gently squeezed. Remi moved the scant piece of fabric to the side and was shocked to feel bare flesh. "Do you wax or shave, baby?"

Her eyes flew open, a flash of mortification in them which morphed into heated desire when he fingered her clit. "I-I . . . um . . . wax."

Gray nibbled her ear. "Damn, I can't wait to see that."

"Sorry, brother. But you'll have to wait. We're pulling into the MGM." But they weren't there just yet. He curved his fingertips and pushed into her wet entrance. Abby gasped and spread her legs a little further. Their little secretary might be shy around them most times, but when she was receiving pleasure from them, she let her body override her mind—an excellent quality in a submissive.

The limo made a left turn into the driveway of the casino,

and Remi reluctantly pulled his hand from Abby's heat and straightened her skirt for her. Making sure she was watching him, he licked her juices from one finger and then the second one. "So delicious. I'm looking forward to making a meal out of your sweet pussy, Abby." Her jaw dropped, and he chuckled. "You better get used to dirty language because I tend to be quite crass at times when I have a hard-on and can't do anything to relieve it. That and I love how you blush when I talk dirty."

The limo stopped, and the door next to Remi was immediately opened by a valet. He climbed out, then turned back, offering Abby his hand. "Come, little one. I'm starving."

He chuckled to himself at the unintended innuendos. *Oh, yes. Cum, little one.*

GRAY TUCKED Abby into his side as his brother flanked her other side, holding her hand. While she was still blushing a lot, she seemed to be more relaxed as they strode down Fremont Street. The one glass of wine they'd allowed her to have at dinner had probably helped. They hadn't wanted her to have more than one—her responses to them had to be real and not alcohol induced. Thankfully, she'd sipped it and still had a little left at the end of the delicious dinner. The chefs and staff at Joel Robuchon's—the owner and head chef had been out of town—had done a fantastic job with their meal and service.

In awe, Abby's gaze flitted all around, trying to take in everything at once. Fremont Street was one of those places that had to be experienced in person to get the whole effect. The bustling pedestrian mall filled with shops, casinos, restaurants, and street performers was five blocks long, and under a ninety-foot-high, barrel canopy which was actually a video screen. After the sun went down, the free shows began. At the top of each hour, the lights on the strip were turned off and an amazing, six-minute video presentation, set to some of the greatest rock songs of all-time, began. It drew in over seventeen million tourists each year. Tonight, they'd be able to see a dazzling display backdropped by The Who's "Miles Over Vegas," before meeting Edward again and heading back to the MGM in time for the 9:00 p.m. Cirque du Soleil show.

Smiling, Gray realized it had been ages since he and Remi had done something vanilla and fun like this with a woman, and because they were doing it with Abby, it was even more enjoyable. He was vaguely aware of a few curious stares at their touchy-feely threesome, as well as several interested glances and flirtations thrown his and Remi's way, but none of them mattered. Abby did it for him in every way. He knew without a doubt she was the missing link they'd been searching for. They'd been stupid to make her off limits all these months, but then again, if they hadn't, she may very well have run off into the night, never to be seen again. Since becoming their secretary, she'd seen them almost every day, and while she was still shy around them, they were also familiar to her now. Hopefully, that would make the transition into a committed relationship easier for her.

A mime stepped in front of them, causing them to stop short. Dressed in traditional black with a white painted face, the man made an "O" with his mouth. He pointed to Abby and made a voluptuous female shape with his hands, then with a slight of hand, pulled a fake bouquet of flowers from his sleeve and handed them to Abby with a deep bow at the waist. She thanked him with a laugh which warmed Gray from head to toe.

Moving on, they strolled down one side of the mall and up the other. At one little shop, they each got a fried Oreo after Abby admitted she loved them but hadn't had one in a long time. In another store, she picked up a few small souvenirs for her dads, and Remi took the bag from her to carry.

A glance at his watch told Gray they had about five minutes left before the lights dimmed and the overhead show began. Beside him, Abby paused and his head swiveled as he zeroed in on what she was staring at. There was a store display with glass figurines hanging from a Christmas tree behind the window. "What is it, little one?"

She sighed. "I love hummingbirds, and that blue/green one is gorgeous, but I swore I wasn't going to get anymore since I'm running out of room for them in my apartment."

Behind her, Gray's gaze met his brother's and Remi nodded. Once the light show started, Gray would distract her while Remi ran into the shop to get the hummingbird she'd pointed out. It wasn't an expensive, Swarovski or Waterford crystal figurine, just a cheap glass one, but the wistfulness in her voice couldn't be ignored. Christmas was only three weeks away, so they'd tuck the little bird in with other gifts for her.

The thousands of neon lights flashed once then went out completely, plunging the mall into a momentary darkness before the overhead screen lit up the night. The music began as every tourist stopped in their tracks and tilted their heads back to watch the show. Abby was like a kid in a candy store, her gaze going from one end of the video screen to the other, and didn't notice when Remi took a step back and disappeared into the shop behind them. Gray moved her in front of him and wrapped his arms around her waist, holding her closely. He was thrilled when she relaxed against him.

By the time the show was over, Remi had rejoined them, and they made their way through the once-again-moving crowds, to where Edward was waiting. The chauffeur saw them approach and immediately opened the rear door for them. As they'd done earlier, Gray got in first, Remi last, with Abby in between them—that was where she belonged so they were both able to touch her and protect her.

As the vehicle pulled away from the curb, Gray turned toward Abby. Her face was lit up in delight. "Having a good time, little one?"

She nodded. "Yes! That was amazing! And I can't wait to see Cirque du Soleil. I've always wanted to go to one of the shows in Florida, but never had the chance."

"Well, if you enjoy this one, there's a different show in Orlando. We'll have to make a weekend of it soon."

Her smile faltered and her gaze fell to the floor. Gray glanced at Remi and saw the same confusion he felt showing on his brother's face. He gently put his fingers under Abby's chin and forced her gaze to meet his. "What's wrong, sweet Abby?"

"I-I don't know. I guess I keep waiting for the other shoe to drop, as they say. Why the sudden interest in me?"

Remi put his hand on her knee and squeezed. "It's not that we're suddenly interested in you, Abby, although it might seem that way. I, for one, was attracted to you the moment I met you."

"The same goes for me," Gray added. "But up until now, we had an agreement between us that all BDR employees were off limits."

"Then why am I here?"

"Because we finally realized we were both fighting a losing battle when it came to you. You have no idea how much I look forward to seeing you every day. You light up my day, every day."

"Mine, too." Remi's hand slid up her thigh. "I know this relationship will probably be far different than anything you've ever experienced before, but it can work, if you're willing to give it a try. You've had a few hours to think about what you read, and you must have some questions, right?"

She nodded and blushed. Beside her, Gray grinned. "How about this? For every question you ask tonight about the lifestyle and the relationship we want with you, one of us will answer it, then follow it up with a kiss. And I'm not talking about a peck on the cheek, but a toe-curling kiss."

A giggle escaped her. "That's definitely an incentive." She took a deep breath and let it out slowly, clearly thinking of what she wanted to ask first. "Okay, um . . . have you always dated the same woman?"

"Almost always," Remi replied, beating Gray to the punch. "There were a few girls in high school and college we dated on our own, but toward the end of our second year in college we were introduced to the lifestyle by a Domme friend of ours. She thought we would both enjoy it and was right. That's when we realized how much we enjoyed topping a woman together. I don't know how to explain it other than we both felt like we were two halves of a whole, but a ménage gave us an emotional bond we'd never experienced before. Giving a woman pleasure at the same time, increased our own pleasure. Maybe it's the twin thing for us; other ménage duos may feel a different connection. Whatever the reason, it just felt right that first time and has ever since. Once in a blue moon, I've topped a woman at a club without Gray present, but it was usually only for one evening or weekend when he was out of town. He's done the same. But we've known since that first threesome we'd want a permanent ménage with the woman who would make our lives complete."

He leaned forward, his lips descending on hers. Gray's cock hardened as he watched Abby kiss his brother, and he couldn't resist brushing the back of his hand over her breast.

Her bra had no padding, and he could feel her stiff nipple through the fabric.

After a few moments of inhaling their little secretary, Remi released her. "Sorry, I smeared your lipstick." His grin said he wasn't sorry at all.

"That's okay," Abby responded breathlessly. She reached up and thumbed some of the red from his bottom lip. With every interaction with them, she seemed to be gaining a little more confidence. "I can fix it before we get out."

"Next question," Gray prompted. "So I can get my kiss before we get to the MGM."

"Um . . . uh . . ." She shook her head. "No, I can't ask that . . . um—"

He cut her off. "Can't ask what, Abby?"

Her cheeks flamed brighter than they'd been all day. "When you . . . um . . . you and Remi are, you know . . . in . . . um . . . bed with a w-woman, do you . . . um . . ."

Gray's confusion at what she was trying to ask was interrupted by his brother's barked laughter. "I get it! I believe what Abby is trying to very politely ask is if you and I have sexual relations with each other when we're with a woman."

"With each . . . oh, hell no!" His chuckle turned into a full-blown belly laugh, as tears filled his eyes. It took a few moments to recover from before he said, "I'm sorry, Abby, but that's the funniest thing you could have asked. I have absolutely no interest in an incestuous relationship with my brother."

Her relief was evident as an adorable, embarrassed smile appeared. "Well, how was I supposed to know? Remember, I'm new to all this."

He wiped the last of the amused wetness from his eyes, then reached out and cupped her chin. "Oh, I remember, sweetheart. And I'm glad, because I want Remi and I to be the ones to open your eyes to a whole new experience of being pleasured by two men who will worship and cherish you. Now, you owe me a kiss."

Closing the distance between them, he took possession of her delectable mouth. He didn't have much time as they were approaching the MGM resort, so he swiped his tongue over the seam of her closed lips, urging her to open for him. When she did, he plunged inside, tasting and teasing. He held her head still as her tongue danced with his. A moan came from deep inside her and he felt it in his groin. As much as his cock throbbed, wanting to thrust into her pussy, it would have to wait. They didn't want her to think this was a fuck and run for them. Seduction was one of the keys to unlocking her desire for them, the other was trust. She was just starting to relax, and if they moved too fast tonight, they might frighten her with their lust.

Gray felt the limo take a left, and he reluctantly ended the kiss. Thankfully, Remi hit the intercom and told Edward to give them a minute before driving up to the valet. The limo stopped out of the line of traffic and idled. Gray reached over to a small box of tissues on a shelf under the vehicle's bar, and handed one to Abby. "Fix your lipstick, little one, so I can look forward to messing it up again later."

CHAPTER SEVEN

Following the sales clerk through the boutique, Abigail's gaze darted from one stunning evening gown to another, wishing Gray and Remi weren't right on her heels because she wanted to look at the price tags. This was the appointment Remi had made on the phone yesterday when they'd arrived at the hotel. She didn't want to pick a very expensive dress since they were paying for it—not that they couldn't afford it, but she didn't want them to think she was greedy. It was kind of like going to dinner on a first or second date and not picking the most expensive item on the menu.

She'd woken up this morning just as she'd finally gone to sleep last night—alone. After the show, the men had instructed Edward to drive down the Vegas strip to let Abby get the full experience, before heading back to their hotel. They took her back to the suite, escorted her to the master bedroom door, took turns giving her a kiss goodnight, then sent her to bed. It had been far less than she'd expected. While she'd been anxious about sharing a bed with them, she realized as she settled under the covers she would have preferred that to sleeping alone after all the attention they'd given her. It'd been an anti-climactic ending to a wonderful day, and had left her wanting . . . needing that connection to them. Had they changed their minds about a relationship with her? Now that she'd had a brief taste of the Mann brothers, she wasn't sure she could go back to being just their secretary.

They passed a display case filled with jewelry, and she highly doubted any of the large, brilliant stones were cubic zirconia. The shop was located in one of the high-end hotel/casinos, and they'd had to be buzzed through a secure door with a guard standing by. After being told about the appointment this morning over breakfast, she'd expected she'd go alone—what guy wants to go dress shopping with a woman? But they'd told her they wanted to help her find the right gown. She guessed they didn't want her to embarrass them by picking something they would consider dreadful. Although, there didn't appear to be any ugly dresses in the place.

The pretty, size-two blonde named Penelope opened a door toward the back of the shop and ushered her three clients inside. Abigail glanced around in awe and confusion. The room was beautifully decorated with plush carpet, a couch, two wingback chairs, a chaise lounge, several cherry wood tables, and elegant wallpaper. Above it all, a huge, chandelier hung from the vaulted ceiling—and she swore it was Waterford. The entire setup could be a living room in a rich person's mansion instead of an area in a boutique. On a buffet, there was a bottle of champagne chilling in an ice bucket, three crystal flutes, a cheese and fruit platter, and chocolate covered strawberries. The only thing that looked out of place was the rack of dresses in varying lengths and colors along one wall.

As Remi and Gray sat and made themselves comfortable,

the clerk poured the champagne and handed a glass to Abigail before giving one to both men. "I've chosen a large selection in the size you requested, however, if you don't find something you like among these, there are more I can bring in." She pointed to a small box on a side table next to Remi's chair. "If you need anything else, gentlemen, please push the button on the intercom, and I'll return."

On the couch, Gray crossed an ankle over the opposite knee. "Thank you. That'll be all for now."

With a professional air, the woman nodded and then left them alone, closing the door behind her. Abigail stood in the center of the room, taking it all in, feeling out of place. Remi sipped from his glass, then indicated the one in her hand. "Don't you like champagne, little one?"

There was that endearment again. Abigail had never in her adult life felt "little" but next to the hulking, broad-shouldered Mann brothers she did, especially when they called her the new nickname it appeared they'd chosen for her.

"No . . . I mean, yes, I do." She took a sip, hoping the alcohol would calm her nerves. It was the best champagne she'd ever tasted—not that she had a taste of the bubbly often, but damn, it was delicious. She took another sip as she stepped over to the rack of over a dozen gorgeous gowns. "I . . . um . . . are these the dresses I should choose from?"

"Yes. They should all be in your size. I'd love to see you try on that one on the right end first."

Her gaze fell on the robin's egg blue and silver gown—it was stunning, shimmering under the soft light from above. She looked over her shoulder at them. "H-How did you know my size?"

A sexy grin appeared on Gray's face as his gaze roamed her body from head to toe and back up again. "Some men just know what size their woman is, Abby. It comes from spending a lot of time admiring her beautiful curves."

What? There was so much about those two statements that made her head spin. She swallowed hard as a shiver went down her spine at the way they were staring at her. *Their woman? Beautiful curves?* Obviously, he'd been speaking in general terms and not about her specifically. Or maybe he had. They'd been so attentive last night and again at breakfast this morning, seemingly oblivious to other women who had flirted with them. Abigail hadn't been oblivious, but the brothers hadn't acknowledged any of them beyond what had been necessary to be polite, before returning their attention to her. "Um . . . okay. So, the blue one first."

After setting her glass down carefully on the coffee table in front of the men, she grabbed the hanger and lifted the gown off the rack. Sure enough, it was a size 12. Glancing around, her confusion returned when she only saw the one door which lead back out to the main boutique. "Uh . . . where's the dressing room?"

"You're standing in it, little one," Remi told her with a smile.

REMI DID his best to hold back his laughter at Abby's incredulity. If he let it loose, the shopping expedition may not go as planned.

"Th-This is the dressing room?" One would think they'd told her the dressing room doubled as the White House's Oval Office by the expression on her face.

"Yes, little one. I've already had my hand on your pussy, so having you strip down to your bra and panties isn't an unreasonable request. If you think it is, you have your safeword. Do you remember what it is?"

She shifted on her feet nervously. "Y-Yes, it's . . . um . . . red."

"Very good. Rule number one was you must verbalize your responses to our questions. Rule number two is if we ask what your safeword is, or indicate in some manner that we're in D/s mode, or we're in our club, that is when we want you to use the title 'Sir' or 'Master.' Otherwise, we like you to call us by our names. Are you comfortable with that?"

"Yes, Sir."

If she were an experienced sub, neither one of them would say anything at this point, letting their silence drag on until she realized they were waiting for her to undress or use her safeword. It had been a long time since they'd played with an extreme novice to the lifestyle, and they had to remember to take baby steps. That didn't mean they weren't going to nudge her beyond her comfort zone. "Okay, now you have two choices. Either strip down to your underwear and try the dress on or say your safeword." He gave her an impish smile. "But if you say red, I think I might be on the verge of dying from curiosity again."

Despite her obvious nervousness, the corners of her mouth ticked upward at his teasing. She placed the dress back on the rack, and her hands shook as they moved to the buttons of the emerald green blouse she'd paired with a black pencil skirt and "fuck me," black high heels. He loved when she wore those; they made him want to bend her over his desk, slide the snug material up to her hips, and take her from behind.

Remi's dirty thoughts were interrupted by Gray standing. "I think Abby needs a little help, brother. Otherwise, we'll be here all day."

His twin stalked across the room and stood behind a wide-eyed Abby who'd barely undone two buttons while Remi had been fantasizing. Gray took hold of her wrists and gently guided her hands down to her sides. His fingers then went to work on the buttons of her blouse, giving Remi a show, revealing one tantalizing inch of her at a time. The edges of a pale green, lace bra came into view over her rounded breasts, and her breath hitched. Gray closed the distance between him and Abby, and was evidently rubbing his erection against her bottom as he opened the last few buttons. Abby shivered as he dragged the fabric down her arms.

Damn, she's fucking beautiful. Without being subtle, Remi adjusted the throbbing cock in his pants. There was no hiding the fact he was hard as a rock, not that he wanted to. Abby did this to him incessantly, and it was about time she knew it.

Gray laid the blouse over the back of a nearby chair, then returned his attention to Abby. He cupped her breasts, which fit perfectly in his massive hands. Massaging them, he pulled her against his chest. "Put your arms up around my neck, little one."

She did as she was told while Gray began to play with her nipples through the thin material. With his nose and chin, he nudged her hair to the side so he could nuzzle her neck. He murmured Remi's earlier thought. "You're so fucking beautiful, Abby."

Her smile fell, and she opened her mouth to say something, but Remi stopped her. "Don't, Abby. Don't you dare say whatever made you frown. Rule number three—you will never, *ever,* put yourself down. Women come in all shapes and sizes, and despite what the fashion magazines say, most men like some meat on their women. Why the modeling industry and Hollywood went from women like Marilyn Monroe and Sophia Loren to skinny twigs is beyond me. We like curves and lush, spankable asses. So, this is your last warning. The next time you're about to say something negative about yourself, you better think twice, because I guarantee you'll end up over one of our laps for a spanking you won't like."

Her mouth slammed shut as Gray chuckled behind her. "I think we better give our sexy secretary a pleasurable spanking before she earns a punishment one."

Remi grinned. "I agree. I have a feeling she's going to be a challenge at times." His gaze went from Gray's to Abby's. "And that's not a bad thing, sweetheart. You're an intelligent, competent, sexy woman, and you'll keep both of us on our toes. But that also means we'll be keeping you on yours, too. Now, come over here."

When she hesitated, Gray's mouth went to her ear. "You can say your safeword at any time, little one, but I think you'll enjoy this . . . especially when we let you cum afterward."

Her chin whipped around, and she almost knocked Gray on his ass with the sudden movement. "I-In here? What if the salesclerk comes back in?"

Gray took her hand and led her over to Remi who moved to the couch his brother had vacated so they'd have more room. "She'll only come back in if we call her or there's a fire. No worries about that. Now, lay down across my lap."

Abby bit her lip and slowly took a step forward, but Gray stopped her, his hands going to the side zipper of her skirt. "Hang on one second. This needs to come off anyway for you to try on the dresses." He made quick work of the zipper, and pushed the skirt to the floor, then held her hand for her to step out of it. "Damn, thigh highs again. I think that's going to be a new dress requirement for the inner office staff."

Blushing, Abby giggled. "You do know I'm the only inner office staff you have, right?"

"Oh, yeah. I'm very aware of that. I'll write up a memo

about the thigh highs when we get back to Tampa. Down you go." He gently pushed against her back.

There was only one final, split second of hesitation before Abby placed herself across Remi's lap. He helped her get comfortable, resting her upper body on the couch. Gray lowered himself and took a seat on the floor beside her head. She shivered and her skin pebbled with goosebumps under their touch. Through her anxiety, though, Remi had seen the burning desire in her eyes. She wanted this . . . had fantasized about this . . . needed this. And he was so looking forward to giving it to her.

His hand started at the band of her stockings and trailed sensually up to her bare cheeks. *Thigh highs and a thong? Lord have mercy!* "Have you ever been spanked before, Abby? As an adult, of course."

"N-No, Sir."

"Mmm. Good girl using Sir." He squeezed one cheek and then the other. "I'd hate to have to turn this into a punishment. I'll start off light, then make them a little harder so you feel the sting. Try to push past any pain and feel the heat. If things get too much and you want me to slow down, just say the word yellow. If you can't take it anymore, say red. But don't worry, my intent is for you to get turned on, not off, so you shouldn't need to say either safeword."

After Remi nodded at his brother, Gray leaned over and kissed her bare shoulder. "Repeat your safewords for me, little one, so I know you remember them."

Before she had a chance to say either word, Remi slid his hand between her legs and over her wet heat. She was already hot and bothered, and they hadn't even started yet. She gasped and squirmed. "*Oh! Ohhmmmm!*"

Both men chuckled, and Gray lightly bit her shoulder. "Safewords, Abby. What are they?"

"Uh . . . um . . . red and . . . and yellow, Sir."

"Good girl." Remi picked his hand up and tapped the left side of her ass. She startled but remained on his lap. He knew it hadn't hurt, far from it, but he would increase the intensity as the blood came to the surface of her flesh and she relaxed a little more.

Another slap landed on her right cheek and he felt the anxious tension fade from her body as it was replaced with lust. Gray was rubbing her back, nibbling on her ear, and whispering sweet nothings to her. After several more spanks on her curvy backside, Remi began to up the heat factor. The next slap came down hard, and Abby yelped and bucked her hips. When he massaged the spot and held the warmth in, she moaned, and the sound went straight to his groin. On the floor, Gray shifted, giving his own hard-on some growing room.

Abby's shoulders relaxed again, and this time he slapped her other ass cheek. Each spank was harder than the last, and she cried out after each one, but her moaning, panting, and gyrating hips told him she was turned on by it all. Gray slipped his hand between her and the couch, down into her bra. She turned slightly to give him easier access, and his brother grinned. "I think it's time to get her off, Rem."

"My pleasure." Rubbing her sore ass with one hand, the other went between her legs again. "Fuck, she's soaked. You liked that, didn't you, little one?" Without giving her a chance to respond, he pushed aside the scrap of fabric that was her thong and plunged two fingers into her core, her heat burning him. "Well, you'll like this even more."

The two brothers worked in tandem, taking her higher and higher. Remi finger fucked her and squeezed her ass cheeks, while Gray played with her tits and kissed her. Abby's hips thrust upward, and one foot fell to the floor, opening up for Remi even more. Faster and harder his fingers assailed her pussy, and he felt her walls start to quiver. "She's close, Gray. Let's send her over."

Finding her G-spot, his fingers rubbed it furiously. He spanked her hard, once then twice, and the orgasm hit her. She screamed into Gray's mouth, muffling the sound for the outside world. She clenched around Remi's fingers, almost crushing them. His thumb found her clit and pressed down hard, sending a second wave of ecstasy through her. His hand was coated with her juices.

As she floated back down from the heavens, she quieted, and Gray lifted his head with a satisfied grin. "I think dress shopping is my new favorite thing to do."

CHAPTER EIGHT

"Who knew I could go to Paris without ever leaving the US," Abby said in awe as the limo pulled up to the Paris Las Vegas Hotel. A half-scale replica of the Eiffel Tower loomed overhead. The first pre-award party they were attending tonight was being held at the Parisian hotel's Chateau Nightclub & Rooftop. They had two other parties along the strip they'd be stopping at before heading back to their own hotel.

After Remi and Gray had rocked her world in the boutique's dressing room, and she'd recovered from two amazing orgasms, the three of them had unanimously agreed on the blue and silver dress for her to wear tomorrow night to the awards ceremony. The men had picked out jewelry for her as well, while she'd found a stunning pair of silver stilettos at the shoe display. Whilst Remi paid for everything, Gray had distracted Abigail, so she had no idea what everything had cost. She was sure she would've had a heart attack if she'd been allowed to see the receipt. There hadn't been any prices on the tags she'd been able to sneak peeks at. Apparently, everything had been computerized.

Once the items had been secured in the limo, their daytime driver, Luann, took them off the strip to another boutique. That one had specialized in vintage clothing. Before entering the first shop for the gown, Gray had asked the female chauffeur to find a store which specialized in retro clothes for them, and Abigail was blown away by the twins' attention to detail. They remember things she'd said she liked, and it hadn't taken them long to agree on a dress similar to the one she'd worn the night before. Gray and Remi had both said they loved her hour-glass figure in the 50s era cut.

The hem of this dress landed just below her knees, and it had a red underskirt with a black layer partially draped over it. The top portion was a black halter, tied behind her nape, with the color running down the outer curve of her breasts then under them to her waist and below. The dark color offset the red cups with the sweetheart neckline covering her breasts, a bow sitting between them. It was fun and flirty, and since Vegas had gone country for the weekend, she'd paired it with the black, cowgirl boots she'd packed. They were new, and she'd only worn them once before, so they were in perfect condition to wear to the parties.

Gray and Remi were holy-hell handsome in their chosen attire. Gray was wearing black jeans, black cowboy boots, and a steel gray, button-down shirt. She'd teased him earlier that it was the first time she'd seen him dress for his name. Meanwhile, Remi had donned blue jeans, a black T-shirt, black boots, and a black sports jacket. His two-day beard and mustache, still hiding the bruise on his jaw she hadn't asked him about, completed the look. Her men were drool-worthy as usual. And, yes, for at least this weekend, they were *her* men. She'd deal with the possibility this fantasy would fizzle out and end on Monday, when she returned to Tampa.

Edward, their chauffeur for the evening again, pulled up

to the valet, and one of the attendants opened the door. Before any of them climbed out of the back of the limo, the paparazzi and fans gathered behind ropes started taking pictures like crazy, without even knowing who was about to emerge. Abigail was amazed at the frenzy, and this was just for one party. There would be more at the other two being held at different hotels. "Is it always like this?"

Remi climbed out and then held out his hand to help her. "It depends. Sometimes it's a little tamer, and sometimes it's worse. Just smile and ignore the vultures and you'll be fine."

"Remi! Grayson! Who's your date?"

"Was she the cause of your breakup with Aurora?"

"Look this way!"

"Remi!"

"Did Aurora catch you cheating?"

"Gray! This way!"

"What's her name?"

"What's your name, sweetie?"

Abigail was shaking in her boots at all the yelling, questions, and demands, but the hotel guards kept everyone behind the ropes, and Gray and Remi closely flanked her on the way inside. One's arm was around her shoulders, the other's around her waist. Camera flashes came at them from almost every angle, and a twenty-something woman even lifted her shirt and displayed her bare breasts for the twins, who ignored her. She was quickly escorted away by security.

As the doors shut behind them, the din died down a little. At least in here, the noise was from the party-goers and music. Before leading her into the club, Gray brought her hand to his lips. "Are you okay, little one? I'm sorry, we should have prepared you for that. We forgot you've never had to deal with this side of things before."

Taking a deep breath, she let it out slowly. "I think I'm

okay. I just need a minute and maybe a drink to calm my nerves."

Remi grinned. "Gray can give you the minute while I fetch us drinks. Wine, champagne, or something else?"

"I-I don't know. Um . . . surprise me."

Something about her request had Remi's smile widening. His eyes filled with . . . with something she couldn't figure out. Adoration? Pleasure? Love? No, definitely not love. She'd only been with them for less than two days—hell, they hadn't even slept together yet. Love wasn't on the radar at this point. Well, whatever it was, he was happy and that made her happy. He placed a kiss on her cheek, his coarse whiskers rasping against her skin. "Can't go smearing your lipstick this early in the evening. I'll meet you two inside."

As Remi strode into the club, Gray leaned down and whispered in her ear, "He's pleased because you trusted him to make the drink choice for you. I know it sounds like something really simple and insignificant, but a Dom takes great pleasure in taking care of his submissive. We want to provide for you, pamper you, pleasure you, and simply be with you. That's what makes us happy, sweet Abby. Well, that and your orgasms."

He stood straight again and winked at her. "Ready to go inside?"

Smiling, she nodded. "Yes. Just don't leave my side. I'm nervous enough as it is."

"Trust me, Abby. At no time will you be left unattended. If that happened, as hot and sexy as you look, we'd be fighting men off left and right. Either Remi or I or both of us will be attached to you all night, unless you have to use the ladies' room, of course. But if you need us in there, we'll make it happen."

Relaxing a little more at his teasing, she let him lead her

toward the doors of the club. "I think I can handle the ladies' room on my own, thanks."

"If you insist."

As they entered the club, the volume increased again. Conversation, laughter, and drinks flowed. Abigail immediately recognized several famous celebrities and country music singers. There were even a few from other genres present, and everyone seemed to be having a good time. They found Remi paying for a round of their drinks at the bar, and he handed her a flute of champagne. Gray took a tumbler of whiskey from his brother and waved at someone across the room. Abigail turned to see who it was.

Summer Hayes ran over with a huge grin on her face. The twenty-eight-year-old, short-haired blonde was another one of BDR's bestselling country artists. However, unlike Aurora, Summer was as sweet and amicable as she could be. She always took time to chat with Abigail anytime she was at the Tampa offices, and had even taken her out to lunch one afternoon while on a break from a day of recording.

The petite singer was wearing a white, country-styled, lace dress with brown, western boots. She looked like she was ready to walk down some lonely, back road and film a music video for one of the fun, upbeat, or sultry songs she'd become famous for. Squealing, she threw her arms around Abigail. "Oh, my God! What are you doing here? Did these two brutes finally wake up and see what was under their noses all this time?"

Confused, but happy to see a friend there, Abigail hugged her back. "What are you talking about?"

Laughing, Summer let her go and rolled her eyes. "Please. I've seen how they ogle you when they think no one's looking. And you only stutter when they're around so I figured the feelings were mutual. And don't try to tell me you're only here because they needed a date. Remi and Gray don't play games like that." She winked at the men. "Although, they do like to play other games."

Leaning down, Gray, then Remi gave the woman a chaste peck on the cheek. The latter tweaked her nose. "Brat. You can explain that statement to Abby. In fact, I think you better before she thinks the worst of us. She's a newbie."

Summer's eyes widened. "So you told her? Cool." She turned back to Abigail and lowered her voice so she wouldn't be overheard. "No worries. I wasn't insinuating I'd ever played with these two hunky Doms—I haven't—but I'm a sub in the lifestyle if you have any questions. Of course, that's not publicized. When Remi and Gray figured out I played and was afraid to go into any lifestyle clubs after my first album started climbing the charts, they investigated several private clubs all over the US. They found me places where I could either hide my identity or trust the members wouldn't out me to the press. I'm not ashamed of who I am, but it has the potential to tank a career."

Abigail was stunned at the revelation. "I never knew."

"That's the great thing about the community—privacy is cherished and respected. Sometimes I'll run into someone I've met at a club out in public. We pretend we know each other from somewhere else. So, back to what I said earlier, if you have any questions, you have my phone number.

"By the way, love your dress!"

The little pixie could change subjects faster than a jackrabbit sometimes, and it took a moment for Abigail to adjust. Before she could say or ask anything more, several people joined their little group. Most of them were in the entertainment industry, and the topics switched to business and tomorrow's award nominees. She knew more people there than she'd thought she would, having met them at the main BDR offices before, or spoken to them on the phone.

Gray and Remi introduced her to anyone she hadn't met

yet or couldn't remember who they were. The twins were never far from her side. It seemed like most of the time, one or the other or both were touching her in some subtle way, letting her know she was on their minds, despite the distractions of the party crowd. There were heated looks, light caresses, a wink, a sweet kiss, and more. By the time they'd done all three parties, then headed back to their hotel, it was close to 1:00 a.m. During the return limo ride, she'd shared several passionate kisses with both men, which had left her wanting more. Now, Abigail was so turned on, she prayed on the elevator ride up she wouldn't be sleeping alone tonight. She didn't think she could handle it if they escorted her to her bedroom door and left her for their own beds.

An idea began to form in her mind. Now, if only she had the courage to follow through with it.

GRAY TRAILED after Abby and Remi out of the elevator. They'd told Fergus earlier they wouldn't need any services when they returned for the night, so the evening butler had left hours ago. They had the place to themselves.

His gaze followed Abby around the living area as his brother flopped onto the couch. "What a night! Gray, I'm shocked you didn't punch that jackass at the second party. I guess he didn't realize that self-important arrogance is the fastest way to turn off a potential investor. What the hell was he trying to sell?"

He shrugged. "I don't even remember. I tuned him out after the first two minutes."

"You lasted longer than I did . . ." Remi paused to yawn. "I tuned him out after a minute."

It had been a long evening, but aside from that one idiot, it had been a lot of fun. And having Abby by their sides had been the icing on the cake. Once she relaxed after running into Summer, she really seemed to enjoy herself. She'd held her own in many conversations and made positive impressions on people she'd never met before. One country artist from another music label had gotten into a lively debate with her about baking, of all things. The twins had laughed when the women had exchanged email addresses to share their favorite recipes.

Thankfully, they hadn't run into Aurora tonight, but there would be no escaping the woman tomorrow night. One of the awards she was up for, Album of the Year, meant her producers would be expected to take the stage with her if she won. It was the first time Gray hoped their artist didn't win in a category.

Abby stood with her back to the room, looking out at the balcony and the neon lights of the strip. Gray strode over and wrapped his arms around her waist. "Are you tired, sweetheart? It's been a long day."

"Not really. But I would like to get out of this dress."

He was about to suggest she go to her bedroom and put on some pajamas, then rejoin them for a nightcap, but her hips shifted and she rubbed her ass against his groin. An involuntary groan escaped him as he felt himself grow hard. "Hmm. Remi, I think our sexy secretary is feeling frisky."

"Awesome." His brother didn't sound as tired as he had a few minutes ago.

Gray took a step back, and his fingers untied the halter from Abby's neck, then found the dress's zipper, slowly sliding it downward. "The dress can go, but keep your boots on for now. Lacy underwear and cowgirl boots sound very naughty. And right now, I'm in the mood for naughty."

"Yes, Sir," she answered breathlessly.

His cock lengthened in his jeans, struggling to find some room. Since she'd called them sir at the office for so long, it shouldn't surprise him how quickly she'd adapted it in response to their dominance. He slid the dress down her body, letting it pool at her feet. Taking her hand, he led her back to where Remi still lounged on the couch. Before either of the twins could say anything, Abby lowered herself to the floor, bent her head forward, rested her ass on the heels of her boots, and then placed her hands on her thighs, palms up.

"Fuck me," Remi whispered in shock.

Gray felt it, too. While this was what they'd hoped for one day with her, they hadn't expected it so soon. His mouth watered at the sight of her. "Did you learn how to present on the website or from Summer, Abby?"

The women had taken several shared trips to the ladies' room during the course of the evening, and Gray had no doubts the subject of their conversations had veered towards the lifestyle more than once or twice. Several times, Abby had returned to their sides with a bright blush on her cheeks. Right behind her had been Summer with an amused grin spread across her face.

"A little of both, Sir. Am I doing it right?"

"You're doing it perfectly, my sweet." Stepping behind her, he unclasped and removed her bra, tossing it to the side. Forget what he'd said earlier, he wanted her naked. Squatting down, he said, "I'll buy you a new pair," then ripped the thong from her body, causing her to gasp.

"Damn, that was hot," his brother said, chuckling. "I'll buy her a thousand thongs just to watch you rip them off her every night. Let her keep the boots on, though. The phrase 'cowgirl up' is running through my head."

Gray reached around and cupped Abby's breasts, feeling the weight of them before squeezing. His mouth found her ear, and he kissed and nibbled it. "You started this, little one, but before we go any further, make sure this is what you really want. You can always say your safeword if you need to.

We won't be mad, but the way your body is responding, I don't think you want to say it. So tell us, baby, what *do* you want."

A shiver went down her spine. "I-I'm not sure, Sir. I do know I don't want to go to bed alone tonight. But I'm also very nervous."

"Understandable." His fingers rolled, and plucked her nipples as his brother watched silently. She arched her back, thrusting her breasts out for him. "There's so much we still haven't discussed, so we'll take things slow and easy, until you've had a chance to complete a limit list. Would you be comfortable giving Remi a blowjob, while I eat your sweet pussy, then fuck you until we're all exhausted? No tying you up, flogging, anal, or anything else that will be on a limit list; just good, old-fashioned, dirty, oral and doggie-style sex." He trailed one hand down her torso and between her legs where he found her wet and hot. His fingers glided through her swollen folds as his other hand continued to tease her nipple. "Would you like that, Abby? Or you could say your safeword, and we could just cuddle in bed and go to sleep. But I think I can speak for Remi when I say we don't want you to sleep alone tonight, either."

He flicked her clit, and she gasped then moaned. "Pleassse."

"Please what, baby? Talk dirty to us. What do you want?"

"Um . . ." She swallowed hard, seemingly at a loss for words as her head fell back onto his shoulder.

Standing suddenly, Remi strode toward the stairs. "I'll be right back. Keep playing."

Gray had a feeling he knew what his brother was up to, so he continued to stroke the burning embers of Abby's desire as Remi practically ran up to the second floor. Dipping one finger, then two, into her vagina, he used his thumb to strum the side of her clit. His other hand skimmed downward and around to her back, where he grabbed her ass cheek. Her hands closed around his forearm which lay against her abdomen, and her hips started to undulate. He tightened his hold on her, keeping her immobile. "Stay still and let me play. Reach up and put your hands behind my neck. Keep them there."

When she did as she was told, he squeezed her ass. "Can you feel where Remi spanked you earlier? I love that it turned you on, you naughty girl. You're so incredibly beautiful and sexy, yet shy. That gets me so fucking hard, but I want to bury my face in your sweet pussy for hours before I fuck you." Panting, she moaned as his fingers tortured her clit and thrust in and out of her core. "You like dirty talk, don't you, baby? It makes you so fucking hot and wet."

His finger rubbed the base of her spine, dipping an inch or so between her ass cheeks. "When we get back home, we're going to start prepping this fine ass to take one of us, while the other is fucking you here." He plunged his fingers deep inside her cunt and held them there as he ground the heel of his hand against her mound.

She cried out. "Please! Oh, God, please!"

Coming back down the stairs, Remi rejoined them. He'd shed all his clothes with the exception of his boxer briefs, which were barely restraining his erection, and in his hand was the blindfold from the plane. "Had to search the pockets of your luggage. Was about to say fuck it and rip up one of your shirts."

"Of course it would be one of mine." Gray smirked. He pulled his hand from between Abby's legs as Remi tossed him the blindfold, dropped some condoms on a nearby table, then went to the suite's control panel to turn on some music. Sensual jazz filled the room.

Covering Abby's eyes, Gray made sure the strap was comfortable on her head and not pulling her hair; that was his job. Grabbing a handful, he tugged her head back, and his mouth descended on hers. This time there was no hesitation from her, and she parted her lips, granting him immediate entry.

In front of her, Remi sank to his knees and sucked one of her nipples into his mouth as his hand disappeared between her legs. Abby gulped, and her moan vibrated around Gray's tongue. Leaving her mouth, he kissed and nuzzled her jawline and neck. "I'm still waiting for you to talk dirty, sweetheart. What do you want to do? What do you want *us* to do?"

"Oh, God, you're . . . you're doing it. *Ahhh.*" Whatever Remi had done with his mouth or hands had caused her to buck her hips.

"Uh-uh, baby," Gray said. "Not good enough. Tell us what you want or we'll stop everything until you start talking dirty." He gently bit her shoulder. "Come on, you naughty girl. I know you have it in you."

Another moan erupted from her. "*Ummmmm* . . . I . . . uh . . . want you to f-fuck my . . . my pussy while Remi . . . while I give Remi a . . . a blowjob."

He chuckled, then licked her ear. "We'll have to work on that, but for now, when you say our names during play, it'll be Master Remi and Master Gray, or Sir."

"Okay, Master Gray."

"Good girl."

Standing, he quickly undressed, then lay down on the couch. "Abby, come sit on my face and let me at that pussy of yours."

Remi stood and took her hand, helping her to her feet. Her pussy glistened, and her nipples were distended and stiff, which made Gray even harder. With Remi's assistance, she climbed on top of Gray and settled down on his face. Her scent was intoxicating and his tongue attacked her with fervor.

"Ah!" Her hips flexed, and he wrapped his hands around her upper thighs holding her in place. Instead of trying to get away, she ground her pussy against his mouth. A combination of sweet and spicy coated his taste buds, as he thrust his tongue as deep inside her as it could go. His thumb found her clit again, as he sucked on her swollen folds.

Next to the couch, behind Gray's head, Remi stripped off his briefs. "Lean forward, baby, and take me in your mouth."

Her weight shifted as she bent her head, and Remi cursed. "Fuck! That feels incredible. Damn, baby, your mouth is hot. Take as much as you can, then suck me hard."

The sounds of heavy breathing and moaning filled the air. Gray's lips moved upward and closed around her little clit. His tongue lashed at it, and she screamed around Remi's cock, her orgasm surprising them all. Her juices covered his chin as she shook from the intense pleasure. As much as he wanted to send her over the edge with his mouth a second time, his dick needed to be inside her, and there was more than one way to make her cum again.

Lifting her up on her knees, he slid out from under her. Remi handed him a condom, which he quickly donned before kneeling behind Abby. Her head bobbed up and down as his twin fucked her mouth. Remi's hand was in her hair, setting the pace he wanted her to take. His eyes were shut, his head back in obvious pleasure.

Gray lined his cock up with Abby's slit, gliding the tip over it several times before easing into her. She was so wet, his invasion went smoothly as he advanced further with each thrust of his hips. The drag of her walls against his hard flesh was sheer heaven.

Reaching down with his other hand, Remi pinched and teased her nipples. Her hips rotated against Gray's pelvis as he buried himself deep inside her then stilled, making sure he didn't shoot his load too soon. When he got himself under tentative control, he began to fuck her. The fingers of one hand rubbed and scratched her back, while the other held her waist tightly. He set a pace in time to Remi's. "Damn, little one. So fucking tight . . . so fucking beautiful."

A deep sense of connection to her flowed through him, unlike anything he'd ever experienced before. She was their woman, and they would mark her as such tonight. She owned their hearts, bodies, and souls.

Adjusting the angle of his hips, Gray pounded into her, his shaft hitting that magical spot, deep in her core. A tingling began low in his spine at the same time he noticed Remi shorten his thrusts and speed up. They were both close, but Abby had to go over the edge with them. His fingers found her clit, rubbing it hard and fast. "Cum for us, sweet Abby. Cum now!"

Her walls clenched around him, milking him, as he saw stars and came inside her with one final thrust. Remi roared, shooting his seed down her throat. While she swallowed some, more seeped out from the corners of her mouth and rolled down her chin. She was breathing heavily through her nose and released his cock to gasp for more oxygen.

Remi stumbled back a step, then reached for Gray's discarded shirt. He wiped the cum from her face as Gray slid from her core. Out of breath, he smirked at his twin, who swiped drops of semen from the leather arm of the couch with the shirt. "You're cleaning that or explaining to Fergus why it's got body fluids on it." Leaning forward, he kissed the back of Abby's head and removed her blindfold. "That was amazing, baby. Are you okay?"

She collapsed back against his chest with her eyes closed. "Mm-hmm."

Laughing, he stood, made sure she wouldn't fall, and quickly discarded the used condom in a wastebasket next to the computer desk. They'd done her in. With one arm behind her back, he tucked the other under her knees and lifted her. She gasped at the weightlessness and grabbed him around the neck. "I-I can walk. Put me down."

With Remi following, Gray strode toward the stairs with her in his arms. "Hush. You're not as heavy as you seem to think you are, little one. When I want to carry you, keep that pretty mouth shut and relax."

When they reached the master bedroom, Remi pulled the bedspread and sheets down, and Gray laid her in the middle of the mattress, then removed her boots. Climbing into the bed with her, the brothers sandwiched their woman between them. Within minutes, they were all asleep.

CHAPTER NINE

Abby was more nervous tonight than she'd been last night on the ride in the limo. This was her first red-carpet moment, and she prayed she wouldn't trip and fall flat on her face in front of everyone. On either side of her, the twins were dressed in their custom Boss tuxedos. They were handsome in regular clothes, but the formal wear made them downright gorgeous. She'd be the envy of every woman there tonight, she knew, and once again, uncertainty swamped her. Reaching up, her fingers played with one of the blue sapphire, drop earrings they'd picked out for her. A matching bracelet was wrapped around her wrist right above the emerald-cut ring on her left middle finger.

Taking her right hand, Remi brought it to his mouth and kissed it. "Nothing to worry about, little one. There will be a lot more security here tonight and the paparazzi will be on short leashes. The fans will be far back, behind the ropes. We'll be stopped along the way for pictures and some interviews; just follow our lead and smile. You look dazzling; you'll knock 'em dead."

She smiled and blushed. "It's the dress and jewelry." The

pale blue, floor-length gown, with sparkling silver trim, hugged her curves. The top of it was sleeveless and strapless, but dozens of thin silver strands went from the sweetheart bust line to a choker collar around her neck, leaving her shoulders and upper back bare. Her hair was swept into a romantic looking updo, with a few loose curls framing her face. The silver stilettos she'd chosen completed the look and added four inches to her five-foot-six frame.

"Uh-uh. It's you. The dress and jewelry just accent your beauty."

"Did you enjoy the massage and stuff this morning?" Gray asked.

While the brothers had run out to do a few errands after breakfast, they'd made an appointment for her at the hotel's luxurious day spa, and she'd spent three hours there being pampered. A full body massage had been followed by a facial, mani/pedi, hair styling, and makeup application. When the women had finished and spun her around to face a mirror, she hadn't recognized herself. Today was the prettiest she'd ever felt in her entire life. But it wasn't just the makeup and the updo. It was Remi and Gray.

Last night's sexual escapades had been followed up with another one this morning. She'd woken up with Remi between her thighs, licking her like an ice cream cone. Gray had joined in, sucking her breasts. It hadn't taken her long to cum for them. Remi had then fucked her in bed missionary style, before Gray had brought her into the shower. There was a tiled bench in there where he'd sat, turned her around, and entered her from behind. He'd bounced her off his lap repeatedly until they both yelled their combined release. She'd never known she could have multiple orgasms, but the brothers made sure she did.

Their limo slowly made its way through the long procession of vehicles dropping off their elite passengers.

When their turn came, Remi got out first then helped her exit. As Gray joined them, there were shouts for them to look at the cameras, however, there were no rude questions as there had been the night before. They posed for pictures along the red carpet and were stopped by an *Entertainment Tonight* reporter for a brief interview. Abby wished she'd known in advance because she would have set her DVR to record the evening, celebrity news show back home. It would be her first time—and maybe her last—on television, and she wanted to save it.

It took about fifteen minutes for them to get past the fanfare and into the Mandalay Bay Resort & Casino's Event Center where the awards ceremony was taking place. They were escorted to their seats: fourth row, center. Summer and her manager sat in the first two seats from the right aisle, two rows ahead of them. Meanwhile, Aurora, escorted by a good looking man Abigail had never seen before, sat in the front row to the left of center. And if looks could kill, Abigail would be on the way to the morgue. Aurora was seething as she glared at her settling in between the Mann brothers.

Gray squeezed her hand as other country celebrities took their seats around them. "Ignore her. She's nothing to be jealous of, and I completely regret our time with her. I just wish we'd stopped fighting our attraction to you long before now."

Tearing her attention away from the bitch in high-heels, Abigail waved at Summer and gave her a thumbs up. Like Aurora, the songstress was up for several awards tonight, and Abigail hoped she won every one of them.

The show started with a large opening number featuring several artists, before the host and hostess took the stage. There were the usual jokes and roasting of celebrities, and then the first category was awarded. When a country band performed via a live feed from another resort, Abigail headed to the restrooms with a few other women. As she entered the opulent lounge, someone grabbed her arm and spun her around, almost sending her on her ass.

"So Remi and Gray are slumming it—with their fat secretary, of all fucking people," Aurora spat at her. The lounge chatter suddenly ceased, and all eyes focused on them. "Don't get too attached to them; they'll be crawling back to me soon."

Fury filled her, but before she could do or say anything in response Summer appeared by her side, dressed in a stunning, black and white gown. "Don't even dignify that with a response, Abigail. She lost out on a good thing, and she knows it. Take a hike, Aurora. Oh, and nice body shaming. Haven't you heard? Bullying is frowned upon these days."

Aurora's eyes flashed with rage at her interrupted harassment. "You bitch!"

Shrugging her shoulders, Summer took Abigail's arm and turned her toward the line for the lavatories. "Good luck tonight, Aurora. You'll need it. But win or lose, you'll never win back Remi and Gray. They've found the real thing, and she's a classier woman than you'll ever be."

Dismissing the other woman, Summer joined Abigail in the line as Aurora stormed out the door. "Sorry if I stepped on your toes by interrupting, but you looked like you wanted to take a swing at her, and that wouldn't have been good. It would have been all over the internet before the ceremony was even over.

"Oh, and by the way, you look freaking gorgeous tonight. I wish I had curves like you. Remi must have picked the dress out."

Confused and trying to change speeds with the petite woman again, Abigail furrowed her brow. "He did, but how did you know?"

"Blue is his favorite color, and don't act like you don't know that. You wear more blue than any other color at work. My guess is you discovered it was his favorite about a month after you started as their secretary. I was in Tampa then, recording, and one week, I think you wore something blue every day." She giggled. "It took those two knuckleheads enough time to discover what was right in front of them. Don't let bitches like Aurora ruin what you three have together. It's obvious to everyone here tonight, Remi and Gray only have eyes for you."

By the time they'd headed back to their seats, another award had been handed out and the winners were finishing their acceptance speeches. Abigail and Summer waited for the ushers' signal for them to take their seats so the cameras wouldn't catch them returning. Abigail felt the last of her anger toward Aurora fade as she saw what Summer had said was true. Remi and Gray's eyes lit up like Christmas trees when they saw her. There was no place on Earth she'd rather be, aside from their bed, than sitting between them. As they had the night before and throughout the day, every chance they had to touch her, wink at her, or whisper in her ear, they took.

When it came time for the Female Artist of the Year award, Abigail grasped both men's hands and prayed. Summer's number one hit, "Broken Tears," had already won Best Single by a Female Artist, and she was now up against four other women, including Aurora, for this award. Aurora had won Music Video by a Female Artist and Music Video of the Year, however, she'd lost Album of the Year, to Abigail's relief. That had been the award Remi and Gray would have been expected to accept with her on stage.

Country music legend George Strait stood at the podium and announced the female nominees, before opening the gold envelope. "And the winner is . . ." A huge grin appeared on his face. "Summer Hayes!"

The audience burst into applause as a stunned Summer hugged her manager, who was sitting beside her, then walked toward the stairs leading to the stage. Tears filled her eyes as she accepted the crystal statue and began to thank everyone who'd helped her get to where she was today, including Remi and Gray. Abigail was so happy for the woman she was coming to think of as a friend, and didn't even bother looking to see the disappointment that had to be on Aurora's face. The bitch didn't matter to her. Summer had been right; what had been Aurora's loss was Abigail's gain, and there was no way she was letting Remi and Gray go unless she had to.

STRETCHED out on one of the jet's couches, Abigail's head rested on a pillow on Gray's lap as he stroked her hair while watching one of the *Fast and Furious* movies on the TV. Remi's eyes were shut as he relaxed in a nearby recliner, but she knew he wasn't sleeping because his hand was caressing her bare foot. It had been a long whirlwind of a weekend, and she was nervous about what would happen when they landed in Tampa. Neither of them had said a word about continuing the relationship they'd started once they returned home, and she was afraid to broach the subject. So much had changed in the past few days, and yet, there were things she wanted to remain the same.

Gray picked up the remote and muted the movie. "Okay, little one, what's on your mind? I can almost hear the gears in there churning up smoke."

Instantly alert, Remi stood, grabbed her calves, lifting them, and then sat down, resting her legs on his lap. "Rule number four or whatever number we're up to—I lost count —communication is very important to a relationship. So what's wrong?"

Sighing, she kept her gaze on the clouds outside the window opposite the couch. "What happens when we get home? I love my job and don't want to give it up."

"What made you think we'd ask you to, Abby?" Gray asked softly. "We love seeing you at the office. The only thing that's changed is we'll be seeing you away from there, too. To be honest, we've been waiting for the right time to ask you to move in with us."

"What?" Astonished, Abigail sat up quickly and swung her feet to the ground. Her gaze went back and forth to the two men grinning at her. "M-Move in with you? Just like that?"

Remi took her hand and squeezed it. "Just like that, sweetheart. Don't look so surprised. It may have taken a while to figure out what was right under our noses, but you're it for us, Abby. When we get home, we'll swing by your apartment so you can get some clothes and whatever else you need." He paused, his smile faltering. "Unless that's not what you want. If you need time to think about it, you can have it."

Abigail's mind was spinning. They wanted her to move in with them. Was that the first step to a forever relationship, or would they one day get tired of her and kick her out of their bed and their business? Neither of them had mentioned the word love or marriage. Hell, how did a marriage like that even work?

Standing, she paced back and forth while they silently watched her. Her fathers once told her that if you took a chance, something good might happen or something bad might happen, but if you didn't take the chance, nothing happened. Finally, she stopped in front of them. "Can we slow down just a little? I want to say yes so badly, but I still feel like I'm waiting for you to realize I'm not what you're looking for. Could we . . . I don't know . . . date for a bit?"

"Absolutely. If that's what you need and want, then you'll have it." Gray held out his hand to her, and when she took it, he pulled her to stand between his legs as Remi got to his feet and embraced her waist from behind. "But know this, I could spend a hundred lifetimes with you and never tire of seeing you, touching you, and pleasing you every day."

Remi smiled against her neck. "Not sure when my brother became a poet, but I doubt if I can top that. However, the same goes for me, Abby. If you need time, you have it. But that doesn't mean we're going to stop what we've started. When we get home, you'll fill out a limit list, and we'll start the process for you to be allowed to accompany us to our club. We won't be able to play there until you've been vetted, but you'll be able to observe and learn. Are you okay with all that?"

Relieved, Abigail relaxed into their arms. "Yes . . . Sirs, I'm very okay with that. Thank you."

On the table next to him, Gray's phone chirped with a text message for the third time during their conversation. The first two he'd ignored, but now he picked the phone up and checked the message. His brow furrowed. "Rem, grab the laptop. Summer says 'all hell has broken loose'–whatever that means—and we need to check the entertainment news."

As Abigail sat down next to Gray, who was signing into Twitter on his smartphone, Remi pulled his laptop from its case and booted it up. Gray found what was going on faster than his brother and cursed. "Fucking bitch! I'm going to strangle her!"

"What?" she asked, trying to see the small screen. Remi cursed as well and turned the computer around so Abigail could see it. "Oh. My. God! W-What?"

All over social media were pictures of Abigail, Remi, and

Gray that were taken over the weekend—that wasn't the problem. What had them all shocked was how every article was about the three of them being in the BDSM lifestyle, stating they were involved in deviant sex acts when they went to the club they belonged to—The Covenant.

"Fuck!" Remi spat as he dialed a call on his own phone. "Ian, Devon, and Mitch are going to be fucking pissed!"

Shaking her head at all the hashtags and vile comments she was seeing associated with the articles, tweets, and posts, Abigail asked, "Ian . . . Ian Sawyer? Why will he be pissed?"

"Ian and his brother and cousin own The Covenant. It's a very private, elite club we belong to, and one of the things they hate is the media."

Abigail paled. "Oh, shit. My fathers are going to see this."

As Remi stood and paced while he apologized profusely to Ian Sawyer, Gray pulled Abigail into his arms and closed the laptop, tossing it aside. "I'm so sorry, sweetheart. This has to be Aurora's doing, but we'll fix it. We'll talk to your dads, and all this will be old news after a few days. But there's no way you're going to your apartment now. I'm sure the paparazzi will be parked out there soon, if they're not already. You're coming home with us. For now, let me call the PR department and have them start on damage control. Then we'll get increased security at the house and office."

After nodding, she lifted her chin and kissed Gray on the lips. This wasn't their fault at all, and she didn't want them to think she blamed them. She'd deal with her fathers later—they were on vacation in Bermuda anyway—but for now, there was work to be done. "I'll call PR. I am, after all, your secretary, and this is what I do best."

A sexy grin spread across his face. "Oh, I can think of several things you do better. In fact, once we take care of all of this, I'm going to ask you to do a few of them."

CHAPTER TEN

Abigail paced back and forth in the hallway outside the twin's home office. The door was closed, and they'd been in there for over twenty minutes talking on the phone with her dads. Remi, Gray, and she had just arrived at the twin's mansion when her cell phone rang. When she burst into tears at the sound of both their voices over the speaker phone, Gray had taken her cell from her, and told her folks he'd call them back in a few minutes after making sure Abby was okay. That was about a half hour ago. Apparently, they were having a man-to-man-to-man-to-man conversation.

The door swung open, startling Abigail. Her hand flew to her chest as she let out a loud yelp. Remi smiled at her and held out his hand. "Everything's fine, sweetheart. Percy and Steve want to talk to you."

Percy and Steve? Gray had called them Dr. and Mr. Turner thirty minutes ago. The four-way conversation must have gone better than she'd expected. It wasn't every day your two dads wanted to talk to your new ménage partners, who you also happened to be madly in love with. Yup, she was in love with them. The support and caring they'd shown her over the past few hours had cemented in her mind what she already knew in her heart. Yet, she still didn't know if they felt the same.

Taking Remi's hand, she let him lead her into the office. Gray was sitting behind the massive, wooden desk and stood. "Sit here, Abby. Your dads are on the speaker phone. We'll step out while you talk to them." He held the chair out for her and after she sat, he kissed the top of her head. "Steve? Percy? She's all yours. We'll see you when you get home from Bermuda."

Her jaw dropped as her dads acknowledged him. Then Remi winked at her before the two men left her alone. Her eyes began to water again. "Dad? Pa? I'm so sorry. I just—"

"What are you sorry for, baby?" Percy interrupted her. "For being bullied by a woman hell-bent on revenge?"

"For so many things, Pa. What are your friends going to say? And the hospital?"

"Abigail," Steve said. "We don't care about anybody but you. We never told you, but we looked into BDR when you first started working there to make sure you were in a safe environment. And then when you were promoted, we definitely looked into Remi and Gray."

"What?" She had no idea they'd done that.

Percy chuckled. "Of course, we did, sweetheart. We knew all about the BDSM lifestyle they lived. But they're also upstanding citizens. They donate to and are involved in quite a few charities, and they treat women the way they deserve to be treated—with nothing but respect. However, I think they'll be making an example out of Aurora Locke, which is fine with me. We've never mentioned it to you, but we know several people who are in committed, long-term, D/s relationships—we even tried it once when you were little, but it wasn't for us."

Her jaw was almost on the floor. "Oh, please don't tell me who topped who . . . no one wants to hear that about their parents. As far as I'm concerned, you two have never had sex, and don't tell me otherwise." Their laughter came over the line, and she shook her head. "But this is more than a D/s relationship. If I had to choose between Remi and Gray, I couldn't. They're like two halves of a whole, and that whole makes me feel complete. I know this happened really fast, but . . . but it just feels right."

"Then go with your heart, Abigail," Steve said, softly. "We'll stand behind your decision, no matter what it is. Just do what will make you happy. Gray and Remi have told us their intentions, which I'll leave for them to share with you. If anyone at the hospital or among our friends has an issue with it, then that's their problem—not ours, and definitely not yours. We love you, baby. Whatever you decide is fine with us. Just don't make your decision based on what others think. If we had done that thirty plus years ago, we would've never had you—the light of our lives."

That did it—Abigail started sobbing as her dads tried to calm her down. She loved them so much and felt that same love returned to her. No matter what, they had her back and would respect her decision—the decision she already knew she'd made deep inside her heart. She loved Remi and Gray, and nobody . . . *nobody* . . . would stand in the way of her having the life she wanted. But first, she needed to find out if that was the life the Mann brothers wanted, too.

After wishing her dads a good time on the rest of their vacation, she promised they'd all have dinner sometime next week and hung up the phone. When she opened the door, she found the hallway empty and ducked into the nearby bathroom to fix her makeup before going to look for her men.

She searched the entire first floor, calling out their names, with no response or sign of them. Sticking her head out one of the back doors, she also saw the lanai was empty. They had to be upstairs somewhere. Walking to the foyer, she stopped when she saw a trail of red on the white marble tile. There were rose petals scattered on each step of the staircase, leading up to the second floor. *Now where the hell had they gotten rose petals?* They'd come straight here from the airport.

Smiling, she followed the trail they'd left her up the stairs and to the left, down a hallway. They disappeared into the room at the end. One of the double doors was cracked open, but the interior was dimly lit. Pushing open the door, she stepped inside. It was a master bedroom suite with a huge, canopied bed, a fireplace, and sitting area. The decor was tastefully done in greens, burgundies, and golds. At the foot of the bed stood Remi and Gray, and holy hell, they were hotter than Hades. They'd changed out of their travelling clothes and now wore black leather pants . . . and nothing else. Talk about sin on two legs—times two.

The flickering light from the gas fireplace glistened off their tanned skin. Her mouth watered as her gaze went up one pair of leather-encased legs, over a thick bulge in the crotch, past every mesa and valley of carved flesh, and down another, just as hard and turned on, male body. Neither one of them moved.

"Strip completely, then come here, little one," Gray rumbled.

Their heated gazes warmed her, and with the removal of each garment she'd been wearing, her heart pounded faster and faster until she was sure they could hear it across the room. Their repeated assurances of how much they loved her body had eased her shyness about undressing in front of them, but she still blushed as she removed her bra and underwear. She placed them neatly atop her shirt and pants on a nearby chair.

Abigail's legs shook with a combination of anxiety and anticipation, with the latter winning the waging war within her. She crossed the room, took a deep breath, and without waiting for a command, lowered herself to her knees. With her head bent, she sat on her heels with her hands on her thighs, palms up.

A hand gently ran down the back of her head, and Remi said, "Sweet Abby, you don't know how much it pleases us to have you kneel in front of us. I'll have to thank Summer next time I talk to her. She obviously gave you some pointers."

Gray squatted down in front of her and cupped her chin, raising it until she was looking at him. The blaze from the fireplace reflected and danced in his hazel eyes, highlighting their warm, chestnut color. "You're so incredibly beautiful, little one. You take my breath away."

"Thank you, Sir."

His hand swept out in an arc. "This room has never been slept in. We've been saving it for the woman we wanted to spend our lives with. I know this happened fast, but Remi and I now know, this room was built for you to share with us. We love you, Abby. I know we already asked and you wanted to wait, but since you can't go back to your apartment until the media dies down, will you move in with us? Will you be our submissive, our lover, our best friend, and eventually, when the time is right, will you be our wife?"

Abigail gasped at his last word. Her gaze shot from Gray's face to Remi's as he squatted down next to his brother. This was the first time either of them had said the "L" word or mentioned a lifetime commitment, and that's what her heart had been waiting to hear. "I-I . . . are you sure?"

Remi smiled. "We wouldn't have asked you if we weren't one hundred percent positive. But if you need some time to think about it, we'll—"

"No! I mean, no, Sir, I don't need time. I love you both,

too." Tears began to roll down her cheeks as her gaze flitted back and forth between the two men. "Yes, I'll be your submissive, lover, best friend, and . . . and when the time is right . . . yes, I'll be your wife."

Reaching up to the bed, Remi grabbed something and held it up for her to see. It was a stunning, diamond and onyx necklace that had to have cost a small fortune, but that didn't matter to her. It could be cheap glass on dental floss for all she cared. As long as it was from her men, that was all she needed.

"This is the collar we chose for you," Remi said as he showed her the white gold heart in the middle of the necklace with two, small, white gold locks linked onto it. "It was the errand we had to run yesterday morning. I hope you like it."

"I-It's beautiful."

"Just like the woman we chose it for," Gray said as he stood and took the collar from Remi. He stepped behind her and, as his brother held her hair up for him, clasped it around her neck. "We know this might be too fancy to wear to work, so we'll take you to pick out one or two you can wear every day. But each one will have the same meaning—you are ours, and we are yours."

Abigail couldn't resist the urge to finger the collar. She was theirs and they were hers. It was a dream come true.

Standing, Remi offered her his hand. "Come, sweet Abby. I'm dying to finally break in this big bed."

Taking his proffered hand, she stood and eyed the four-poster bed with the wood canopy. It was extra-wide and would easily accommodate the three of them comfortably at night. But what she hadn't really looked at was the wooden "X" at the foot of the bed from the base to the top of the posters. There were empty hooks on either side of it and she wondered what BDSM implements would be hanging there soon. Apparently, this wasn't a bed you could order from the local furniture store or *1-800-Mattress*.

She was pleased to know they'd never brought another woman in here. A few rose petals had been tossed across the pillows and a bouquet of roses stood on each night stand. "Where did you get the flowers?"

Remi bent down and scooped her up in his arms. "I called Kristen Sawyer, or Anders as you know her, from the plane. She's Ian's sister-in-law, by the way—Devon's wife." Abigail had never met Ian or Devon Sawyer from Trident Security, and had only spoken to Ian on the phone—never his brother. "After we found out you wouldn't be able to go back to your apartment, I asked her to send a few things with the guards Ian had sent over." He placed her in the middle of the bed, then pointed to where Gray had retrieved a bag from the dark, wood dresser.

"What other things?" she asked with more than a hint of suspicion and anxiety. The grins on their faces told her whatever was in the bag would result in her having multiple orgasms by the time they were through, but getting there would be interesting and maybe a little uncomfortable.

"Nothing too extreme, little one. Just a few things from the club store." Gray pulled out several items and placed them on the bed next to her. "If anything looks like it might be on your hard limit list or you're not sure what it's for, let me know. And we've entered D/s mode, so every time you forget to use the words Master or Sir, you'll rack up punishment points."

"Y-Yes, Sir. Sorry." She gulped as she inspected the items. Leather wrist and ankle cuffs—*okay*. A vibrator—*doable*. A tube of lubricant and—*what the hell is that?*

"Um . . . what . . . what's that thing, Sir?" She pointed at a pink item.

Remi chuckled. "Anal beads, Abby. I assume you're an anal virgin; no one's taken that sweet ass yet?"

"Yes . . . I-I mean, no, Sir . . . I've never . . . um . . ."

"No worries." He picked up the stiff string of round beads. There were seven of them, each one larger than the last. "We start with the smallest and ease them in until you can't take anymore. Tonight, you'll only get a few of them, but we'll start with that. Then over the next few days, we'll switch over to anal plugs to get you ready for us. You'll be well prepped before that happens."

Grabbing the leather restraints, Gray began to attach them to her wrist and ankles. "What're your safewords, Abby?"

Her gaze followed his hands as he worked. "R-Red for stop, yellow to slow down, Sir."

"Good girl." He tossed the remaining wrist and ankle restraints across the bed to Remi. "Remember, we won't be upset or mad if you say them. In fact, we will be mad if you're hurting or scared and don't say them."

"Yes, Sir."

When Remi finished, he made a circling motion with his hand. "Flip over to your stomach, baby. On your knees, arms straight out, head down, and put that sweet ass in the air."

Nervously, she did as instructed, and he hooked her wrists to a short chain he'd pulled up from under the head of the bed. A hand that had to belong to Gray ran over her bare ass and goosebumps pebbled across her skin.

"Easy, Abby." Gray's voice had dropped to what she was starting to recognize as his Dom tone. Kristen Anders-Sawyer had mentioned it several times in her books, and now Abigail understood why the subs all shivered when their Doms used it on them.

A cool liquid dropped on the crack of her ass, and she startled. Remi sat down on the bed next to her and tapped her knees. "Spread them wide for me, but not so far that you're uncomfortable."

Shifting from side to side, she put as much distance between her knees as she could. A finger ran over her anus, spreading the lubricant. Meanwhile, Remi began to play with her nipples and waxed pussy. She couldn't help the moans and pleas that escaped her. "*Ohhh-mmmm.* Yes, pleassse!"

"Like that, don't you?" Remi asked before nipping her hip then licking away the sting. "Well, get ready for more."

His fingers left her wet core and a few moments later she heard a humming sound. *Oh, shit!*

Abigail barely registered the thought of what was making that noise before the vibrator touched her clit. Her hips bucked as she cried out. Every cell in her body screamed in lust and pleasure, and she barely noticed that the smallest of the beads had entered her ass. Sensations assailed her nipples, clit, pussy, and ass. With a free hand, Gray raked blunt fingernails down her spine. Combined, it was almost overwhelming. Part of her feared the intensity of the orgasm which was building inside her with a fierceness she'd never experienced before. But as her mind and body spiraled out of control, she was poised on the edge of an abyss she desperately wanted to fall into.

Another bead passed her sphincter and that one she definitely felt, but the vibrator suddenly changed in intensity. "Oh, my, God! Please, oh, Sirs! Please!"

"Cum whenever you need to, baby," Gray encouraged. "We'll work on controlling them another night."

She thanked the heavens, because as another bead began to breach her ass, Remi pushed the vibrator harder on her clit, and she screamed as the orgasm crashed over her. Spots danced in front of her closed eyelids as her entire body shook with the force of sheer pleasure. Remi and Gray's hands continued their combined assault and before she could recover from the first orgasm, another one hit her even harder. When they finally let her come down from the intense high, she collapsed onto the bed, gasping for air.

The vibrator was removed, but the anal beads stayed in place. Four hands caressed every inch of her, as lips and tongues kissed and licked her reverently. On one side, Remi lay next to her, whispering sweet words in her ear as Gray climbed onto the bed on her other side. He unhooked her wrists from the chain. "Relax, little one. Let us take care of you while you take a nap. Because when you wake up, you'll need all your strength to keep up with us."

Heaven help her.

CHAPTER ELEVEN

After a knock sounded at his closed office door, Gray stood and strode toward it, trying to keep an evil smirk from forming. *This is going to be so damn satisfying.*

He opened the door, his body blocking the view of the rest of the room, and pasted on a smile. "Hello, Aurora. You're ten minutes late."

Moving closer, she placed her hand on his chest, seduction written all over her face. As usual, she was dressed to the nines. A red miniskirt topped off legs encased in over-the-knee, black boots. Her short-sleeved, black, silk shirt showed an obscene amount of cleavage for a Friday morning business meeting, and she was dripping in diamonds. Thankfully, the twins had never gifted her with any expensive jewelry because she might need to hock it all soon. "You know me, Gray. I love to make an entrance. I'm so glad you called so we can put all this behind us."

She had no idea how ironically true her statement was about to become. Taking a step back, he opened the door wider for her to enter his lair. The singer sashayed in and came to an abrupt stop when she saw all the other people in the room. Remi, Ian and Devon Sawyer, their cousin Mitch Sawyer, Reggie Helm, two of BDR's lawyers, and Abby were either sitting on chairs or the couch, or standing and leaning against a wall. Each one was frowning, and with the exception of Abby, had their Dom faces and attitudes on.

Glancing around in confusion, Aurora asked, "What's going on? Remi? Gray?"

Indicating an empty chair in front of the desk, Remi tapped the back of it. "Have a seat, Aurora. There are some things we need to discuss."

She hesitated, uncertain, and then the bitch was back as she strode across the room and gracefully took a seat. "I'm not sure what this is all about—"

"This is about the end of your contract with Black Diamond Records," Gray interrupted as he crossed his arms over his chest.

"W-Wha-What are you talking about? You can't end my contract!" Her eyes were wide in a combination of incredulity and fear.

"Oh, yes, they can," one of BDR's lawyers, Joe Stillman, responded as he stepped forward and handed her a copy of her contract with the pertinent clause highlighted. "'At no time can the client, herein known as Aurora Locke, bring negative publicity, slander, or liable to Black Diamond Records, its CEOs, Remington and Grayson Mann, or any of their employees or other clients. If that occurs, Black Diamond Record reserves the right to void the representation of Aurora Locke and all recording contracts.' If you notice at the bottom of the clause, your initials are there saying you signed off on it."

"But . . . but, I didn't do anything!" Her indignation was evident in both her expression and the increasing volume of her voice. "I'll sue! You can't prove I did anything!"

"Oh, yes, they can." Ian sneered and shook his head. "The

blood-sucking lawyer and I seem to be the start of a broken record—pun intended."

He hit a button on the TV remote he'd been holding and the screen on the wall next to the door came to life. While the picture jumped around a lot, it was clear the *TMZ* reporter was secretly recording his interview with Aurora, getting the alleged dirty scoop on the Mann brothers, Abigail Turner, and The Covenant. The private, elite BDSM club was now dealing with an influx of applicants, reporters, and curiosity seekers. A pissed-off Ian had already contacted a company to push the front gate fence line a quarter mile to the east, complete with a new guardhouse. With the wooded area surrounding the existing fence, that would help prevent the paparazzi from trying to get covert pictures of the club's members. He was also having Boomer's wife, Kat, train a few more K9s for added security.

Stillman looked down his nose at a sputtering Aurora. "That and the reporter's signed affidavit are all we need to void your contracts."

"Which means . . ." Remi added, " . . . you're no longer a recording artist with Black Diamond Records. That will be announced this afternoon by the PR staff. We've also rescinded your new album. It belongs to BDR and won't be released."

Aurora jumped up, her face beet red. "You can't do this!"

"Oh, yes, they can." That time, it was all the men in the room, with Abby clearly trying not to laugh out loud at them.

Reggie, the Sawyer brothers' lawyer and a club Dom, stepped forward, using that commanding voice all Dominants seemed to possess. "Now, sit down because this meeting isn't over yet." After the stunned singer slowly took her seat again, he handed her a stack of papers held together with a thick, black, document clip. When she accepted them, he said, "Consider yourself served. The Covenant and its owners are suing you—"

Her jaw dropped. "But—"

"Shut up and listen; I'm due in court in an hour. As a guest and temporary member of The Covenant, you signed a confidentiality and non-disclosure contract which you've violated. We'll be seeking in excess of $25 million in damages."

"Tw-Twenty-five m-million . . ." Her astonishment was almost comical as her gaze darted from one person to the next, but none of them were sympathetic.

A devilish grin appeared on Ian's face as he shrugged. "Fences are expensive these days." It wasn't that the Sawyer brothers needed the money, not with a self-made billionaire for a father and their own thriving businesses—it was just sweet revenge.

Reggie turned to Abby who'd been sitting there quietly. "Abigail, do you have a dollar on you?"

She certainly did. Gray had given her one earlier and told her to hold onto it, but hadn't explained why. "Um . . . yes." Standing, she pulled it from her skirt pocket and handed it to the lawyer.

"Thank you." Reggie waved it in the air. "This is your retainer I've accepted. I'm now officially your lawyer."

"O-Okay." Her brow furrowed, unsure of where he was going with this.

Turning back to Aurora, who now had rage in her eyes, he gave her another thick stack of papers. "Consider yourself served, again. Ms. Turner is also suing you for slander and is seeking the sum of $15 million dollars."

"What!" Aurora jumped up again, throwing the papers to the floor, in a full rant. They had a strong case since she'd told the reporter Abby had been in The Covenant and participated in deviant sex acts there, when in fact, Abby hadn't been cleared for admittance to the club, nor had she stepped a foot on the property yet. The owners would attest to that in court. "You've got to be crazy! You're all fucking crazy. I'm not giving that bitch, or anyone else, a fucking dime!"

The Mann twins growled as Reggie rolled his eyes. "That's what they all say until I prove them wrong."

But they weren't done with her yet; Remi was about to add the pièce de résistance. "Oh, and Aurora, you should know I spent most of yesterday on the phone speaking to the top fifty or so recording producers in the world, and as a favor to Gray and me, none of them are willing to offer you a contract for at least the next five years."

Her face reddened in fury. "You son of a bitch!"

She lifted her hand to slap him across the face, but Abby was faster, grabbing her by the wrist and twisting it. "That fucking does it! Don't you ever raise a hand to Remi or Gray. They're mine! And I'll be damned if you touch either of them in anger, or for any other reason, ever again. Now get out before I kick your scrawny ass to the curb!"

Their usually sweet submissive shoved the other woman toward the reception area, and after Aurora huffed and fled, Abby slammed the office door behind her. When she spun back to face the room, every pair of shocked, male eyes was staring at her. She took a deep breath and let it out slowly before her voice went back to normal. "What? Just because I was always shy around Remi and Gray doesn't mean my dads didn't teach me how to defend myself and what belongs to me."

Grins appeared around the room. Ian barked out a loud laugh as Gray pulled her into his arms. Remi stepped forward, sandwiching her between them, and they both kissed the top of her head.

Slapping Remi's back on the way to the door, Reggie said,

"I'm out of here. Looking forward to introducing your sub to mine tomorrow night at the opening. Abby, it was very nice to meet you."

The others filed out after saying their goodbyes, but Gray only had Abby on his mind. "I love you, little one."

The last of her ire had quickly faded, and her gaze softened. "I love you, too, Master Gray." She kissed his lips briefly before spinning around and facing his brother. "And I love you, Master Remi."

"I love you, sweet Abby." He kissed her, then lifted his head and arched an amused eyebrow at her. "What do you say I lock the door, turn off the security camera, and we can show you how much we love you? Maybe start off with a spanking for losing some important file, hmm?"

Her eyes widened as his words penetrated her mind. "S-Security camera? I thought there weren't any cameras in your offices."

As Gray chuckled against her neck, Remi grinned. "We know you did."

EPILOGUE

Swallowing hard, Abigail walked into the lobby of The Covenant with Remi and Gray. Her two appointed bodyguards had remained in their car outside the club. In addition to the flood of media attention, her men informed her that until the serial killer targeting submissives in and around Tampa was caught, she would have bodyguards whenever Remi and Gray deemed necessary.

After seeing the industrial warehouse exterior of the club she didn't know what she expected but found the elegant, Victorian decor warm and inviting. There was a sitting area to her right, and on the left was a reception desk similar to what one would see in a hotel. A large, bald, black man with a friendly smile stood next to a set of huge wooden doors with iron accents.

A beautiful, nine-foot Christmas tree stood tall in a corner, and there were holiday lights and decorations tastefully spread around the room. A large painting of Santa, dressed in black leather, cracking a whip over nine, scantily dressed women wearing reindeer ears, sat on an easel near the front desk. The woman at the far end from Santa's sleigh had a red nose, and the scene was both sensual and comical.

Several people were milling about, some in leather or lingerie, and others in everyday wear, carrying their club clothes in tote bags or duffels. A squeal caught her attention and she turned to see Kristen Anders-Sawyer running toward her with her arms wide open. She'd recognize her anywhere from photos on the author's Facebook page and on the backs of her books. Kristen was one of the people currently wearing lingerie. The red and white teddy and matching underwear definitely fit in with the Christmas season.

Kristen threw her arms around her. "Oh, my, God! I'm so glad you're here! When Masters Remi and Gray told me you were their submissive, I couldn't wait to finally meet you. *Whoops*!" She let a shocked Abigail go, and with her gaze on their feet, she faced the Mann brothers. "Sorry, Masters. May I have permission to gush over your submissive, Sirs?"

Bending forward, Remi kissed the brunette on the cheek. "Merry Christmas, Kristen, and permission granted. That goes for you two as well."

Abigail hadn't noticed the other women who'd joined their small group, and Kristen introduced her. "Abigail Turner, this is Shelby Christiansen and the soon-to-be Colleen Helm. I think you met her Dom/fiancé, Reggie, yesterday. We're the welcoming committee for you. If it's okay with your Masters, we'll take you to the women's lounge so you can get changed." She held up a yellow bracelet for the Doms to see. "I've already grabbed her a visitor's band."

Her mind spun. Kristen had always been so nice on social media, but the way she was acting, one would think Abigail was the celebrity. The warm smiles from the three submissives had her relaxing and getting into the festivities.

Gray and Remi had told her they wouldn't be able to play at the club until her background check and medical clearance had been completed. The yellow band made it clear to the members and staff so there were no misunderstandings.

Handing Abigail her tote bag he'd been carrying, Gray answered, "Thank you, ladies. We would appreciate you getting Abby settled. Master Remi and I will be at the bar waiting."

Shelby, a petite woman wearing a green wig, which matched her skimpy club wear, linked her arm with Abigail's with a huge grin. "Thank you, Sirs. Our Masters are at the bar as well. We'll take good care of your subbie and return her to you after we give her all the club gossip."

Rolling his eyes, Remi chuckled. "Uh . . . no. If you do that, we won't see her again until next Friday. You have fifteen minutes."

As they led her toward the double doors, it was clear the women would be cutting it as close to the set deadline as possible as they chatted and pointed things out to her. The huge doorman tipped his head when Kristen introduced him as "Tiny"—a name that belied his size. Shelby explained the head of security wasn't a Dom, so he wasn't addressed with a title. Tiny grinned at her. "It's nice to meet you, Miss Abigail. Welcome to The Covenant."

"Thank you, Tiny. It's nice to meet you, too."

He opened the door for them with a flourish, and her jaw dropped as she entered the main club. This second floor was in the same decor as the lobby, with deep reds, black, and gold being the primary colors. Brass and wrought iron accentuated the deep mahogany furniture and massive, curved bar. A grand staircase led down to the first floor, which Gray had told her earlier was dubbed "the pit," and the balcony overlooked it on both sides of the open area. At the other side of the second floor, there was a small store on the left, and a double-wide hallway with a huge red ribbon blocking it off, taking up the space to the center and right.

She hadn't realized she'd stopped short and was just staring until Kristen tugged her arm. "You'll get the tour in a little bit. Let's get you changed."

The women led her through a door where two staircases indicated the ladies' and gentlemen's lounges were below them. The elegant decor continued into the ladies' locker room which also had a sitting area, along with toilets, showers, and changing rooms. As the women chatted around her, Abigail got changed into the royal blue, silk camisole and short set her Doms had gotten for her during a shopping trip this afternoon. She smiled as she recalled how the excursion had ended similarly to the one in Vegas. Apparently, the men sought out boutiques where naughty behavior in the dressing rooms wasn't frowned upon.

"Love that color on you," Colleen said to her. "Reggie got me that same set in hot pink."

"I saw it in pink, but Remi loves blue."

A gorgeous, willowy redhead, dressed in a black, leather pantsuit and red, thigh-high boots approached. "Pleasing your Doms already. You'll do just fine, little newbie."

Abigail might be new to the lifestyle but, thanks to the research her Doms had her do and Kristen's books, among others, she knew without a doubt the woman was a Domme. A shorter, plump, dark blonde stood by her side, grinning. Kristen bowed her head slightly at the taller woman. "Mistress Roxy, this is Masters Remi and Gray's new submissive, Abigail Turner. Abigail, this is Mistress Roxy and her bratty wife, Kayla."

All of the women laughed except the Dominant, but it was clear she was fighting the urge. Gray and Remi had schooled Abigail in protocol for most of the day, but they'd also told her most Doms and Dommes understood how nerve-racking it could be for new submissives. As long as she was polite, addressed them before a submissive, and used their titles, she shouldn't have a problem. She bowed her head as Kristen had done. "Good evening, Mistress Roxy. It's a pleasure to meet you and Kayla."

"Where is she?" A blonde whirlwind flew in from the entrance to the pit, wearing a sheer, green teddy that left nothing to the imagination except the little satin triangles between her legs and over her nipples. Her gaze went to the group and zoomed in on Abigail. She ran over and hugged her. "Yeah! You're here. So glad, and don't let that bitch Aurora rain on your parade. Sorry! I'm Angie, Master Ian's wife and sub, and can you tell I hated her? We've heard all about how you kicked her scrawny ass when they canceled her contract. I'm glad those two—"

"Ahem." Mistress Roxy cut her off and raised an eyebrow. "Whatever word you were about to use for Masters Gray and Remi, you might rethink using here in the club."

A dark-haired Domme, also dressed in a black pantsuit that was paired with stilettos, joined them with a laugh. "Come on, Roxy. You know those two were idiots until they realized what was right under their noses. Hello, Abigail, I'm Mistress China. If you hadn't noticed, the word of Remi and Gray's pretty, new submissive has already made it around the club. Welcome."

"Um . . . thank you, Mistress China."

Before anyone could say anything else, Remi's voice bellowed down from the locker room stairwell. "Fifteen minutes is up! Where's my subbie?"

They all laughed at Abigail's jaw dropping. Rolling her eyes, Mistress China grasped her arm. "Come on. Let's go soothe the savage beasts. I'll tell them it was my fault so you're not in trouble your first night here."

Thankfully, the Domme convinced Remi and Gray not to

hold her tardiness against Abigail. The next forty-five minutes went by quickly as she was introduced to many subs and Doms who all welcomed her to The Covenant. Remi had said they'd take her on a tour after the opening ceremony for the new wing was completed. Apparently, with the combination of the unveiling and it being the club's Christmas party, most of the three-hundred-seventy-eight members were present.

Instrumental holiday music floated through the air until there was a squelch of a sound system and then someone tapped on a microphone. Loud conversations mellowed as everyone turned to face the hallway to the new wing on the second floor. Mitch Sawyer stood with the mic in his hand while Devon, Kristen, Ian, and Angie stood on either side of him.

"Can I have everyone's attention, please?" The crowd was reduced to soft murmurs, and the music was shut off. Members filled the bar and balcony areas while others stood on the steps leading down to the pit. "On behalf of my cousins and their wives, I want to welcome everyone to The Covenant's Christmas party. Please give our staff a big round of applause for the fantastic job they did decorating the place." Everyone clapped and there were a few whistles before they quieted again. "As you all know, tonight is the unveiling of the new wing, and we're very excited about it. A lot of planning and design went into it, and Master Parker's construction company did an amazing job. Downstairs, we've added a dozen new, private playrooms, with a variety of themes including a second harem room, a sports locker room, a mafia-themed room, an inquisition room, and there's even a futuristic sci-fi room that's really cool. Well, I think it's cool; the subs might think it's something else."

Chuckles filled the cavernous club. "But the upstairs area behind me is what we're really proud of. As most of you know, because we couldn't hide it from the outside, the new wing has a glass dome over it that can be opened to let the night air and starlight in. This area will be known as the garden because, as you'll see, we've created an Eden in there. When the dome is open, you'll notice there's a thin, mesh netting that's pulled across in its place. While you'll be able to see out, the other side of the mesh is reflective, and as a result, we don't need to worry about any drones or helicopters trying to get pictures of the inside. And with the security business next door, we also don't have to worry about satellite photos."

Ian rolled his eyes. "All right, let's wrap this up so everyone can see the place."

"You just want to get the reindeer races underway." More laughter flowed.

"Yup. So without further ado . . ." He took the oversized scissors Angie had been holding, and with Devon and Mitch grabbing the huge ribbon, they cut it, and the crowd cheered then followed the three Doms into the garden.

It took a few moments in the surge of people for Abigail, Remi, and Gray to reach the new wing. It was gorgeous. Mitch had been right; it definitely looked like an Eden. Play stations were along the outer perimeter, and plants, trees, and shrubbery filled in the spaces between them. A soft, artificial grass covered the floor. Instead of the dark, wood furniture in the bar area, the seats and tables here were more whimsical, reminding Abigail of a resort in the Caribbean she'd gone to a few years ago with her dads. There were even a few striped, canvas cabanas with beds and pillows in them.

Some of the seating had been pushed to the side, and a large area of the grass had been roped off. There were six rows marked with white tape running down the length of it, with each row separated into ten squares. At one end of the rows sat what looked, to Abigail, like saddles of some sort attached to rolling dollies. Beside her, Gray and Remi burst out laughing, and the latter pointed at the contraptions. "Oh, this is going to be good. Be grateful you're not cleared to play, Abby. Those are Sybians. They're the ultimate vibrating toys. You straddle them, like you're riding a horse, and put your pussy and clit over the vibrating pads. You can also attach dildos to them so you vibrate inside and out."

Ian took the microphone from Mitch. "All right, Doms. There are submissives walking around with pens and paper. If you want to enter your sub in the reindeer races, put their name on the paper. Six subs will participate in each race—we're sorry, but female subs only tonight. Each sub will choose a new dildo attachment to ride, and obviously, those are theirs to keep for future play. The way this will work is we'll roll the two dice Master Devon is holding." His brother raised one of the large, pink, furry dice over his head. "Whichever numbers come up, the corresponding subs will move to the next spot in their row. If a pair is rolled then the sub will advance two spaces."

He paused and smirked. "This is when the fun begins. If a sub moves, then their Dom, who will be holding the controllers, will increase the intensity of the vibe. The winner will be allowed to orgasm . . . the losers will be out of luck. Any sub that cums before they reach the end, will have to endure another race. We've already entered the names of the single subs to the kitty, and when they're chosen, we'll give the controllers out to Doms, randomly. While you all get your entries in, we'll start off with six of the unattached subbies."

Sticking his hand into a large ice bucket, the head Dom pulled out six names and the female subs stepped forward. They were given headbands, with fabric reindeer antlers and flashing lights on them, and their choice of dildo attachment.

The Sybians were numbered with racing silks, and a male sub stood behind each one.

Remi and Gray sat on a loveseat, and before Abigail could sink to her knees, Gray pulled her into his lap and laid her legs over his brother's thighs. "We like cuddling with you, little one."

She settled her head on his shoulder. "I like being cuddled by you, Sirs."

Moments passed and the submissives were finally ready to start the race. Abigail was very grateful she couldn't participate. She didn't think she was ready for something so public yet. The races started with a roll of the big dice across the grass. As the submissives advanced, being pushed forward by the male subs, there was plenty of moaning, gyrating hips, and oh-my-Gods. The crowd cheered them on as Doms tossed the dice around the playing area. When Number 5 crossed the finish line, and the Dom holding her remote put it on full blast, the woman screamed as her orgasm hit her.

Abigail didn't realize her mouth had dropped open until Gray gently used his fingers to push up her chin. He nuzzled her ear. "I would suggest we get a Sybian, but I think I'd be jealous of it."

She giggled and kissed him. Leaning forward, she then kissed Remi. "I love you, Masters, and can't wait 'til we get home so I can show you how much."

Remi looked at his brother. "You take her to the locker room, and I'll get the car. It's time to take our sweet Abby home."

~

Thank you for reading *Double Down & Dirty*. If you

enjoyed Gray, Remi, and Abigail's story, please take a moment to review it for other readers.

Ready for *Entertaining Distraction: Doms of The Covenant Book 2*? Get it on your favorite sale site!

Check out my website for the Best Reading Order of the Trident Security series and its spinoff series!

ACKNOWLEDGEMENTS

Thanks to Jessica, Julie, and Brandie – love bouncing ideas off of you!

Thanks to the rest of my beta readers—Charla, Jen, Felisha, Joanne, Allena, Debbie, and Katie!

As always, thanks to my incredible editor, Eve Arroyo!

Thanks to my awesome PA, Maria Celaschi Clark!

Thanks to Judi Perkins from Concierge Literary Design for the kick-ass cover!

Thanks to my fantastic Sexy Six-Pack Sirens Facebook group! I can never thank you enough for your support, shout outs, and friendship. You all are amazing!

AUTHOR'S NOTE

The story within these pages is completely fictional but the concepts of BDSM are real. If you do choose to participate in the BDSM lifestyle, please research it carefully and take all precautions to protect yourself. Fiction is based on real life but real life is *not* based on fiction. Remember—Safe, Sane and Consensual!

Any information regarding persons or places has been used with creative literary license so there may be discrepancies between fiction and reality. The missions and personal qualities of members of the military and law enforcement within have been created to enhance the story and, again, may be exaggerated and not coincide with reality.

The author has full respect for the members of the United States military and the varied members of law enforcement and thanks them for their continuing service to making this country as safe and free as possible.

ABOUT THE AUTHOR

A proud member of Romance Writers of America (RWA), Samantha A. Cole is a retired policewoman and former paramedic who is thrilled to add award-winning author to her list of exciting careers. She has lived her entire life in the suburbs of New York City and is looking forward to becoming a snow-bird between New York and Florida someday. Her two fur-babies, Jinx and Bella, keep her company and remind their mom to take a break from writing every once in a while, to go for a walk, which is the best way to deal with a stubborn case of writer's block.

An avid reader since childhood, Samantha was often found with a book in hand and sometimes one in each. After being gifted with a stack of romance novels from her grandmother, her love affair with the genre began in her teens. Many years later, she discovered her love for writing stories was just as strong. Using her life experiences and training, she strives to find the perfect mix of suspense and romance for her readers to enjoy.

Her standalone novel, The Friar, won the silver medal in the 2017 Readers' Favorite Awards in the Contemporary Romance genre out of more than 1000 entries.

While the original planned stories for the Trident Security series have been completed, they have brought many opportunities for Samantha to spread her wings and bring her readers more characters and stories to love. Look for the Trident Security Omega Team series, the Doms of

The Covenant Novella series, the new Hazard Falls series the upcoming Blackhawk Security series, and more from the Malone Brothers series, in addition to several standalone projects.

Sexy Six-Pack's Sirens Group on Facebook
Website
Subscribe to my newsletter
All Author

facebook.com/SamanthaColeAuthor
twitter.com/SamanthaCole222
instagram.com/samanthacoleauthor
bookbub.com/profile/samantha-a-cole
pinterest.com/samanthacoleaut

CPSIA information can be obtained
at www.ICGtesting.com
Printed in the USA
LVHW010959080820
662366LV00007B/418